Last Rites

The Whitborough novels are a supernatural comedy book series, set in a town based upon Whitby and Scarborough. Whitborough on Sea, for the purpose of the story, is the size of both towns combined, in the same location as Scarborough.

At the beginning of this book, there is a map of Whitborough's old town and harbour area, marked with the names of the most important locations. The map is reproduced at the end of this story, together with a full street index.

Last Rites is the last book in the first series. The conclusion of a story spread across five books. There is death, embarrassment, demons and diarrhoea, and an enormous amount of fighting. For these reasons the books should not be read by children or adults with nervous dispositions.

Alistair Lavers is fifty-seven and is still annoying people. He drives a long black car wreathed in mist and he lives in an old house, full of draughts and spiders. His background is in the arts, the military and the occult. Occasionally, somebody spits out their coffee while reading one of his books.

Last Rites

The Whitborough Novels

Alistair Lavers

Matador
Unit E2 Airfield Business Park,
Harrison Road, Market Harborough,
Leicestershire. LE16 7UL
Tel: 0116 2792299
Email: books@troubador.co.uk
Web: www.troubador.co.uk/matador
Twitter: @matadorbooks

ISBN 978 1803132 389

British Library Cataloguing in Publication Data.
A catalogue record for this book is available from the British Library.

Printed and bound by CPI Group (UK) Ltd, Croydon, CR0 4YY
Typeset in 10.5pt Aldine401 BT by Troubador Publishing Ltd, Leicester, UK

Matador is an imprint of Troubador Publishing Ltd

*Last Rites is dedicated to small shopkeepers,
crafts people and small traders everywhere.*

For press and TV reviews, character and location pictures, Valhalla T-shirts and all things Whitborough, visit **alistairlavers.co.uk**

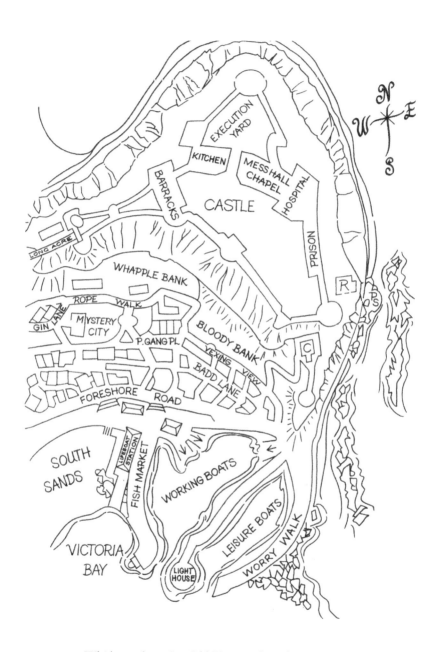

Whitborough on Sea Old Town and Harbour, 1983

Contents

Prologue: I Predict a Riot   xiii

1. Roll Away the Stone, Roll Away the Stone   1

2. If You Go Down to the Woods Today,   14
   You Better Go with a First Aider

3. A Rush and a Push and the Land Is Ours   17

4. As If by Magic, a Shopkeeper Appeared   29

5. Speed Demon   32

6. No Doubt About It   37

7. Very Superstitious   41

8. Rock On   43

9. The Road to Hell, Is Paved with Cake   48

10. Get It On   52

11. You Ain't Nothin' But a Hound Dog   55

12. Set the Controls for the Heart of the Sun   65

13. A Night Like This   71

14. Hi-de-Hi-de-Hi   75
    Ho-de-Ho-de-Howl
    Go, Go, Go, Do the Holiday Rock

15. Synchronicity   84

16. Gangsters   87

17. The Spy Who Taped Me   91

18. The Landkey Sorceress Rides Out   95

19. My People Were Fair and Had Sky in Their Hair...   98
    But Now They're Content to Wear Stars
    on Their Brows

20. Luck Be a Lady Tonight   102

21. Live and Let Die   107

22. Reasons to Be Cheerful, One, Two, Three   109

Photo Credits

Front Cover
Matt Black, as Belator

Inside Front
Cacklog, Chef/Owner of the druids field kitchen

Inside Rear
Clockwise - Albert the Cat, as Brinsley, appears courtesy of
Camilla, on behalf of FOAW (Friends of Animals Wales)
Cai, Betamax, Cadoc and Drydfell
Kawasaki 750H2 appears by kind permission of The
National Automobile Museum of Tasmania.
Dudley Kingcombe, Werewolf (with stick), appears courtesy
of SWFU (South West Farmers Union)

Back Cover
Uther, Director of XXL Druiding - Logistics and Transport

Art Direction and Graphic Design
Alistair Lavers. www.alistairlavers.co.uk

Prologue

I Predict a Riot

Most functional, reliable English folk share a healthy sense of self-preservation and common sense that shields them from the majority of life's many hazards. Unfortunately, the cautious instincts on which we all rely are sometimes severely tested. If a large, apparently untraceable treasure suddenly came into your possession, it might not turn out to be the answer to all your problems. This does not happen very often, but there is enough evidence in our historical records to describe these rare events as a mixed blessing.

Discovering a fortune in gold and jewels without consequence – or a connecting history – can work the most dramatic changes on values and character, changing people so completely that the person their friends and family once recognised has gone. The effects of suddenly finding oneself wealthy beyond imagination is almost like a possession.

Wealth can often magnify anxieties and negative feelings that were manageable and under control. The mind that was once calm and steady now races to action or is overwhelmed by indecisiveness. Plans are hurriedly made then abruptly abandoned. The ability of the individual to suppress their natural flaws or weaknesses ebbs and flows as the ties that bind them are severed in full consciousness, until finally they realise they are adrift, cut off from their inner voice.

This is one such example, but the potential for harm has been magnified by the addition of a double curse, a gunfight and a brawl. Life on the Yorkshire coast has got very exciting very quickly. Especially when you've brought rocket launchers, machine guns and English Civil War-era siege cannons to the gunfight.

To compound the sudden explosion of urban warfare, your county council's mobile librarian accidentally infects the landlord of your local public house with an old werewolf virus on a busy Easter weekend, the local Satanic coven loses a demon, Brinsley the cat and any last traces of their former appetite for ritual conjuring.

So what we've got here, folks, is a right old mess… there is some pain, unavoidable in the circumstances, though fortunately most of it is really quite funny, as long as you cross your legs – whilst you're biting down your nails or looking over your shoulder. Remember that it's only fiction. Or at least some of it is.

Derek Beautimann LLB, partner in law at Beautimann, Buerk and Trippe solicitors, Master of Ceremonies for the Black Hand Coven and budgerigar murderer, had had enough of being the guardian of cursed treasure. He had hoped it would grant him a blessed new life, free of the dull, grinding monotony of conveyancing, petty boundary disputes, contested wills and commercial law – the dull menu of the provincial solicitors across the land. Instead, he'd had weeks of misery, stress, domestic turmoil and the threat of ruination.

He had made up his mind to put it back where it had come from, before the demon who had nearly burned his house down came back to finish the job. At least that part that he alone still possessed, because the rest had disappeared…

On a beautiful warm day, late in May, at around 7am, Derek drove his Jaguar XJS down the long, undulating length of Dickie Hapeknee's Lane, driving south towards the great sweep of the Yorkshire wolds and the distant escarpment, neatly partitioned into blocks of woodland, paddock and farmland underneath the stark outline of RAF Staxton Wold's radar towers. In the bottom of the glacial valley, the York to Whitborough train crawled sluggishly to its terminus, reflecting the sun's rays like a tiny jewelled caterpillar.

Parallel to the railway line, a large flatbed truck rumbled towards Whitborough along the A64, bookended by a Volvo containing four bearded gentlemen and a Mini Metro, carrying three formidable women of a certain age. It was an unremarkable sight as far as the two stationary traffic policeman on duty were concerned, except for the fact that the lorry was carrying a huge stone with a white-haired old man tied down on top of it. Though there was no specific regulation, or law, prohibiting the transport of huge stones with old men tied to them in the Highway Code, his condition of bondage – and its implications for a serious breach of health and safety – would certainly invite an intervention with the law, if there happened to be a traffic patrol car on duty. And so it was, that soon after passing a stationary police car on the A64 outside Rillington, the lorry and its escort was soon shepherded into the next vacant lay-by for further inspection.

Chapter One

Roll Away the Stone, Roll Away the Stone

'Not a lot happening so far, is there?' sighed Sergeant Clifford Dodds, one of Whitborough on Sea's more experienced traffic patrolmen, inside his Ford Sierra. 'Looks like we're going to have another quiet shift. Not such a bad thing, considering the last few weeks we've had. Time for a brew, I think.'

'I'd rather be busy, Cliff. I hate being stuck out here, lurking in bloody lay-bys trying to catch Granny going a few miles an hour over the limit. It's not exactly cutting-edge police work, is it?' grumbled his younger colleague, PC Justin Deighton.

'Why don't you apply for CID then?'

'If only. Me mum and dad said they'd never speak to me again if I even so much as applied to join CID. I'm already on the excommunication waiting list,' replied Deighton, hoping his inspector hadn't let slip that this was exactly what he'd done.

'They don't like you being a copper?'

'That's an understatement.'

'Most folk might say it's a good thing having a copper in the family. I must say, Justin, you and your family get more and more interesting as time goes by, lad.'

'Our family's sole form of income – apart from benefits, black-market fags, booze and dodgy motors – is crime. If I ever got my cards for CID I'd never be able to go home again without an escort.'

'Christmas must be a bit awkward then… you being a pig.'

'The only time any of our lot even wanna look at me is at funerals. Or bloody weddings. Unless they're taking me behind a wall.'

'That's nice for you.'

'To tap me up for advice on how they can play the system. That's the only time they treat me like a human being.'

'So what do you tell 'em?'

'I tell 'em to speak to their brief.'

'You could always move further away. The Met's always looking for kids your age. Plenty of excitement for you down there, lad. Where your family won't find you.'

'I think I'm going to have to move, Cliff.'

'Volvo and a Flatbed coming…' observed Sergeant Dodds. 'Something big behind that cab. Check out that lot behind the bloody windscreen – it's Merlin, Gandalf and Moses… Great beards!'

'That Volvo in front's got four more of 'em inside,' added Patrolman Dodds, taking out a pocketbook.

As the lorry rumbled majestically past their police car the two patrolmen stared in awe at its cargo. A very large oblong stone, which appeared to have kidnapped a very old man.

'Now… that's what I call a *rock*,' gaped PC Deighton.

'There's an old bloke tied down on top of it, Justin. Do you think he's on drugs?'

'A bit hard to tell from here, mate.'

'This should be an interesting conversation. Those women behind in the Metro are a bit close.'

'Maybe they're beard maidens?'

'Oh, very funny.'

'Are we gonna blue light 'em?'

'Too bloody right we are. I can't wait to tell old Marshall about this.'

'He's on sick leave, isn't he?'

'That's just the official line. Unofficially he's still plugged in, so D'Ascoyne said. If I had as much sense I'd have pulled a sickie an' all, Justin.'

'Stick the sirens on.'

Once the three-vehicle convoy was stationary, the younger of the two policemen stepped out from the passenger side of the police car and approached the driver of the truck.

'Do you know why I've stopped you, sir?'

'Hello, how can we help, Officer?' replied Cadoc, the only druid in Whitborough with an HGV licence.

'You could start by explaining why you have what appears to be a live adult male tied to the giant rock you're transporting. He's not what you might call a young man either, is he, sir?'

'He is our chief druid, Officer. As our most senior druid, it is his right to ride those sacred stones which align to the feminine aspect of Mother Earth on their way to their elevation.'

'Elevation?'

'She is on her way to our new henge, to be elevated,' explained Dredfyll, leaning over to the driver's window from the middle of the cab.

'We're planting her big end,' added Betamax solemnly from the left, refusing to meet the eyes of the traffic policeman in case he caught sight of all the pastry flakes in his beard from the two pasties he had gobbled up.

'She?'

'All stones great enough to be raised align to masculine or feminine energy. They reveal their gender from sound vibrations made from a single strike by an iron lance,' explained Cadoc patiently.

'What concerns me, sir, is the safety of the gentleman fastened to it, and his mental state. Is he in some sort of trance?' asked Constable Deighton, looking back at the bearded old man with an obvious expression of disapproval.

'LLOCHRYM, LLOCHRYM, OHMMMMM… LLOCHRYM,' bellowed Pyrlig, the stone's human tuning fork, in an ancient tongue that was one third Welsh, one third fly agaric mushrooms and one third henbane, with mead and honey – to taste.

'A journey such as this is very stressful for sacred stones, Officer,' emphasised Cadoc patiently. 'Our chief druid is now in a deep trance. He has aligned his male energy with the universal fount of cosmic feminine energy in order to balance the latent power of the stone. The ceremonial ropes act as an earth wire to release tension. He must also recite blessings to prevent her from cracking.'

'It's a risk, you see, Officer, even on a double bed of reeds and fleeces,' added Dredfyll, taking a huge swig of mead. 'Just for the nerves,' he added, patting the stoneware flagon as he returned it to his knees.

'Is that an alcoholic drink you're sharing, sir?' asked Constable Deighton, addressing the driver.

4

'It is, Constable, but I've only been drinking Evian,' added Cadoc, holding up a half-empty bottle of mineral water.

'The gentleman behind is not going to be *riding* a great slab of rock – as you put it on this carriageway. You'll have to untie him or we'll be issuing you with a fine to go with the producer I'm writing up.'

'But we're *druids*, Officer –this type of thing is our bread and butter,' snapped Cadoc.

'It's breakfast, dinner and tea too. Menhir planting,' agreed Dredfyll, trying to suppress a burp as he patted his chest. We're heavy rockers… with big rocks.'

'OHMMM! LLOCHRYM, YNYS WHITBROC, LLOCHRYM… OHMMM!'

'His *riding*, as you put it, is a clear breach of health and safety law, the safe carriage of passenger regulations relating to motor vehicles and I have to warn you that you have very likely invalidated your motor insurance.'

'But he's the chief druid, it's traditional…'exclaimed Betamax, propelling more pastry flakes into the passenger foot-well from the hedge of his beard.

'OHMMM!'

'I couldn't care less if he's Uri Geller. I insist you untie that gentleman and transfer him to your cab if you want to continue your journey.'

'But he doesn't want to be untied – he's consented to it! It's the highest honour, riding the stone! Only the most senior members of our order are allowed to ride the stone and she has to arrive on the headland at Cayton bay by 10.30 to prepare,' declared Cadoc.

'The gods demand it!'

'OHMMM!'

'He can't be released, until the stone arrives at her place of elevation... the chief druid must ride the stone. It's a fundamental principle of our religion! He is locked into a deep meditative trance, Officer, the only conduit releasing tension in the stone. The stone is tense, because we have stopped moving; they don't like a lot of stopping and starting, menhirs. It stymies the flow of cosmic energy,' asserted Betamax, turning pink under his crumbs.

'OHMMMMMMMMM!'

'Do you have your transport documentation for the stone, sir?'

Just as things were getting heated, another car pulled in behind the witches' Mini Metro, which the young constable seemed to recognise. His interrogation suddenly ceased as two late middle-aged men in plain clothes got out and walked over to his patrol car. The younger of the two leant down and began to converse with Deighton's colleague but the older man waved his arm at Constable Deighton, clearly indicating he should leave the druids in the lorry and hurry back to his car.

'Stay there, please. I need to speak to my colleague... what did you say you were again?'

'*WE'RE DRUIDS!*'

'Transportation documents... did he mean the scroll, Cadoc, or the depot invoice?' asked Dredfyll, rummaging in the pouch on his belt. 'We have our ceremonial scroll from Ceridwen, she's high priestess of all Powys.'

'He's not here anymore, Dredfyll. Another car pulled up behind our lady witches. He's been summoned for a chat.'

Several minutes passed and then the senior half of the two new arrivals wandered down to the driver's side of the

6

cab. 'Inspector Marshall of Whitborough Police, gentlemen,' announced the older man, producing his warrant card. 'And your name, sir?'

'Cadoc. Son of Cadoc, son of Dinas.'

'Surname?'

'Clark… Robert.'

'Are you the only one driving this vehicle today, Mr Clark?'

'It is my honour, yes.'

'And you two gentlemen?'

'Betamax and Dredfyll. I am the keeper of the sacred mysteries. I hand down the wisdom of our forebears,' explained the more serious-looking man on the left.

'Yes, sir… and your surname, please, if you'd be so kind.'

'Surnames are not used in the druid tradition, Officer.'

'Mercy isn't traditionally offered by traffic patrolman either, sir. Especially to people who flout the Road Traffic Act, the Health and Safety at Work Act, and the safe carriage of heavy loads regulations, sections—'

'*Charles Alfred* Knowles,' replied Betamax resentfully.

'And you, sir?'

'Dredfyll, son of Dredfyll, son of—'

'Just your Christian name and surname, sir, and address, thank you very much.'

'Pete Barnes. Twenty-two Durham St, Whitborough.'

'Can I see your driving licence, Mr Clark? Otherwise the constable will have to give you a producer. I presume *you* haven't been drinking.'

'Only Evian, Inspector. As the gods are my witness.'

'Just a simple yes or no will do – sir.'

'What do you reckon they've stopped us for, Vi?'

'They probably want Pyrlig to get off his rock and sit in the cab.'

'Why, they strapped him on good and tight, didn't they?'

'Best Norfolk reeds and deerskin straps – the silly old fart.'

'That lush young copper's coming over here. Tug your skirts down, girls... actually, on second thoughts leave 'em high.'

'Good morning, ladies.'

'Good morning, Officer – lovely morning, isn't it?'

'Yes, it is...'

'Is there a problem, Officer?'

'We're just trying to resolve a health and safety issue with these gentlemen, ladies, but you're free to continue if you wish. There's no reason for you to wait.'

'Is it old Pyrlig you're worried about?'

'Pyrlig, Miss?'

'The silly old git on the rock. He's been getting strapped to trees and standing stones since he were knee-high to a wheelbarrow.'

'Is that his real name?'

'Yes, it's Welsh...' added Violet, 'as he never gets tired of telling us.'

'May I ask what your relationship is with these gentlemen?'

'Cheeky bastard,' sniped Phyllis... under her breath. 'We're part of their escort, Officer. We're registered witches. Priestesses of Isis.'

'You're witches?'

'Yes, we are,' said Violet, skimming her tongue over her teeth like a Komodo dragon.

'Violet's a traffic warden too, aren't you, Vi?' cackled Joy.

'Aye, she's the best scorer in town,' sniped Phyllis haughtily, reining in the temptation to add she was the best something else too.

'I'll just h-have a word with my, umm, colleague,' said the young policeman with a slight tremor in his voice.

'You do that, lover,' added Violet. 'Don't be a stranger—'

'Tell him we've got to get Pyrlig and his rock to Cayton bay by 10.30, Vi,' hissed Joy from the driver's seat of her Mini Metro.

'WE'VE GOT TO BE AT CAYTON BAY – BY 10.30, AT THE LATEST, OFFICERS!' screeched Violet from the front passenger seat.

'Those two that pulled in behind us in plain clothes must be coppers,' said Joy.

'They're detectives. The younger one got a sword pommel in the forehead in the big brawl I got caught up in at the Saltersgate inn,' said Violet.

'He seems to have healed up.'

'That's Inspector Marshall. The other one,' added Phyllis from the back seat. 'Best policeman they've got in Whitborough. Not like that plonker of a superintendent. D'Ascoyne or whatever his name is.'

'I hope they let us go soon,' muttered Joy.

Inspector Marshall stood close to his colleague, Detective Sergeant Broadhead, but there were no smiles or any detectable warmth between the three older policemen as Constable Deighton returned to their impromptu conference in the lay-by.

'Who are the women in the Metro, Deighton?'

'They say they're *witches*, sir.'

'In the same party, are they, with this lot?'

'Yes, sir.'

'What was she shouting about – that woman in the Metro?'

'They have to be at Cayton Bay for 10.30 for some ceremony, she says.'

'Right, tell 'em to move on and keep their speed under forty as long as he's on the back. Make sure to tell that lot in front in the silver Volvo first. Get to it then, lad, get rid of the lot of' em – *sharpish.*'

'Yes, sir.'

Cyn, Andwearde, Cadwallop and Getafix, the spearhead of the convoy (as much as one can spearhead anything, in a silver Volvo estate), had taken the sudden suspension of their journey with good grace and made the most of their time arguing about the choice of their next cassette, munching through two packets of extra-strong mints as Cyn's homemade Iron Maiden compilation whirred down to the last track. The only other productive thing they had done since stopping was to glance back to Cadoc, Dredfyll and Betamax in the lorry every so often to look for some kind of sign. Apart from a couple of shrugs from their friends behind, they were still none the wiser.

'I hope that young policeman isn't going to detain us for too much longer, I need to go,' groaned Getafix from the back seat.

'Plenty of bushes between here and Cayton bay. The question is, boys, is it Rainbow Rising, Holy Diver or… OH,' asked Cyn.

'OH? Who are they then?' asked Cadwallop from the back seat. 'The support band for Yes?'

'That's "Off the Wall", that is! What a dark horse our old pal Cyn is!' crowed Andwearde in the front passenger seat, as Cyn hastily thrust the cassette box back into the door tray.

'Get Pink Floyd on. It must be years since I heard *The Wall*,' said Cadwallop.

'*Michael Jackson*,' snorted Andwearde.

'EH?'

'*Off the Wall*… by Michael Jackson.'

'MICHAEL JACKSON!'

'IT'S NOT MINE!' protested Cyn. 'It must be my daughter's.'

'Disco dark horse, disco dark horse, disco dark horse,' chanted his companions. 'Don't stop 'til ya get enough!'

'OWW!'

'BUGGER OFF! It's not mine. This is a *family* car. D'you think that *Country Life Magazine* on Andwearde's side is mine too?'

'Calm down. I believe you, mate,' said Getafix.

'I'm putting Dio on,' snapped Cyn. 'Any objections?'

'Good choice, mate,' said Cadwallop, slapping Cyn on the shoulder.

'Keep on – with the force don't stop, don't stop 'til you…' sang Getafix.

'Any more disco-man teases and you can get out and walk, Getta-lift,' growled Cyn.

'Can I have a look through your *Country Life*, mate?' asked Getafix, attempting to make peace with his chauffeur. All three of the others turned to look at him with a slightly concerned expression.

'What's wrong with *Country Life*?' he protested.

'Nothing. Nothing at all,' replied Cyn, shaking his head.

Andwearde and Cadwallop's baffled huffs and clear expressions of pity were almost too much for Getafix, who quickly opened the magazine and buried his face in the lifestyle section.

PC Deighton arrived at Cyn's driver's door window just in time to catch the last rays of an intense look of bewilderment. It was not reassuring.

'My inspector says you can resume your journey, sir, as long as you keep your speed below forty for the safety of the gentleman on the rock. I'm sorry you've been delayed.'

'Good,' grunted Cyn, turning his ignition key with the bare minimum of enthusiasm.

'Safe journey,' mumbled Deighton politely, as the Volvo and its passengers set off without a backward glance.

'It's times like these when I really bloody hate this bloody job,' muttered PC Deighton as he walked back to his patrol car. To cap off the end of his miserable shift, the sassy witch in the front passenger seat of the Mini Metro blew him a kiss before her friends suddenly erupted in a fit of shrieks and cackles.

'Pity we haven't got time to stop for a Mexican at the Parkway,' mumbled Cadwallop.

'There's a barbecue tonight, at the new circle,' said Cyn.

'OH, FANTASTIC, Cyn!'

'BRILLIANT!'

'I could murder a chilli.'

'Me too,' added Getafix, inspecting the lower slopes of his beard for tangles.

'I remember when we had venison burgers at the grove on Landkey Island,' sighed Cadwallop.

'Cacklog always does a good spread, doesn't he? I hope he's doing the barbie,' agreed Andwearde.

'I hear it's pie and peas – on Saturday night, after the stone's up,' added Cyn. 'The queue's gonna be bloody fierce, lads.'

'PIE 'N' PEAS…*OOOOOH!*'

'FOOD OF THE GODS!'

'Let's hope Belator doesn't get in at the head. They'll be none left.'

'Cacklog says it's one pie per beard. One pie per ticket. And nobody's going to argue with a druid holding a big hot spoon full o' molten mushy peas…'

Chapter Two

If You Go Down to the Woods Today,
You Better Go with a First Aider

There are two footpaths to the grass-covered cliff-top plateau overlooking Cayton Bay, three miles to the south of Whitborough on Sea. The higher path drops down through a wood that even most experienced mountain bikers would hesitate to tackle without a full kit of body armour, a good protective piece of headgear and a thick pair of gloves. But even the sycamores and hornbeam, whose low branches and deadly roots had been the cause of so many trail riders' blood-curdling screams, rarely reach full maturity before erosion and gravity conspire to bring them crashing down the treacherous clay slopes onto the beach.

The second footpath, several hundred yards further south, is much less testing and very rarely harmful (unless adders are sunbathing). It is the first choice of those who are fond of the type of coastal walks from which one can expect to return home free of pain and buckled wheels.

Leaf Lane, the lower path, follows an old right of way at the boundary of a large field of oilseed rape and the outer wall of the Cornwallis Holiday Camp, joining the official heritage nature trail marked out by the hardy men and women of Whitborough Conservation Society, who can do great and unusual things in woods with a bolster chisel and a low-velocity mallet.

Both footpaths are regularly pestered by walkers, but the higher path has a very different character at night. 'Creepy' is probably the kindest comment that was ever made about Kenwith Wood after sunset. Some places are just better left… as people say in Yorkshire.

If any outsiders were foolish enough to go there after dark, they could damn well take what was coming to them.

The head of the Black Hand Coven did not look like a classic monster of the woods. Unless you were the kind of person who had a phobia for middle-aged men in Harris Tweed. But under his shirt he did have an exceedingly dangerous hobby – outside of his profession in law. Occasionally, when time, place and the necessary planetary alignments allowed, he liked to conjure demons.

Tall, blond and handsome in his prime and still moderately attractive in a 'best before end date' kind of way, Derek had never had any difficulties attracting a loyal and enthusiastic troupe of like-minded followers, whose enthusiasms leant towards his own. As a clever, educated man with a good speaking voice in a respected profession, his leadership and position was never seriously at risk. He had his fair share of minor quarrels and disagreements with his followers. But this was to be expected. Nothing ever happens in occult circles in Yorkshire without a fight, a lot of sulking and a good deal of plotting.

Because establishing a Satanic coven is such a delicate and secretive business, he had concluded many years before that it was easier to infiltrate and then corrupt an existing club or association of broad-minded people by stealth than start from square one. It was a supremely clever and effective strategy, if the chosen group in question already leans liberally towards alternative lifestyles without the nuisance of any sort of moral foundation.

There was another major advantage in this approach. It gave Derek all the time he needed to appraise the characters and qualities of his new companions and weed out those who were too independently minded, conservative with a small 'c' or not fully on board with the Devil and all his works. All serious opposition could thus be disposed of before he delivered his coup de grâce. In the end, converting the Whitborough and District Isadora Duncan Free Dance Society into the Black Hand Coven was less of a coup and more of a 'friendly' takeover with a little arm-twisting and lots of false promises of the kind so common in the City of London.

Chapter Three

A Rush and a Push and the Land Is Ours

Derek Beautimann, Satan's solicitor, and Maureen Moment, his number two in the Black Hand Coven, drew up on the dark side of Cornelian Drive, north of Cayton Bay, around dusk in Maureen's car and turned off the road, parking in the shadows of the trees on the adjacent area of loose earth and gravel favoured by dog walkers.

'This is the last time I'll be wearing a camouflage jacket and trousers and a ski-mask for you, Derek Beautimann.'

'I think I can say with absolute certainty, Maureen, that neither one of us will be doing this again. Just to reassure you.'

'GOOD.'

'I'm not sitting on wet grass and getting a cold bum either.'

'Are you ready?'

'I am.'

'Let's get rid of this damn gold. Once and for all.'

Two miles away to the south, the joint owners of Clash City Records, Yorkshire's creepiest alternative music and fashion store, drew up in their black Saab 99 Turbo outside Cayton Lanes Holiday Park, taking two short left turns before parking up behind the park's water tanks.

'This is the last time we're dressing up like the firing squad at an IRA funeral.'

'GOOD.'

'I'm not sitting on wet logs and getting a damp arse either.'

'Ready?'

'Let's get rid of it.'

Elsie Cakebread, co-owner of the famous Valhalla Retirement home on Lower Gunstone, walked out of her front door and climbed up onto the pillion seat of her husband's Honda Gold Wing, after putting eight cans of Merrydoome cider in their top box. As carefully as she could, she flattened down her hair and pulled on her full-face helmet, slapping her partner Mark on the thigh once she had connected their sonic intercom to signal that she was ready to roll.

'Else calling Mark.'

'Mark receiving. C'mon back, sexy lady.'

'Cheeky bugger – I'll slap you again.'

'PHWOOAR!'

'Just get this bloody bike to Cayton. We've got druids to see.'

'Did you put the cider in the top box?'

'Yep.'

'Cool. Let's motor.'

The dark grassy plateau in front of the woods above Cayton Bay, which had been the launching pad for all the recent mayhem, was now full of tipsy druids admiring a great bonfire. Some of the more sober members of their society were dutifully patrolling around the edge of a circle of twelve foundation pits with flaming torches, the highest ranking muttered old spells to disperse evil spirits and ensure that the elevation of the new stone circle the next day could proceed under favourable skies. It also meant they could fart and burp to their hearts' content, without drawing attention to themselves, and walk off the hangovers brought on by slurping too much mead.

To avoid any accidents, the foundation pits had been filled with soft, springy hay and the remaining hay bales had been arranged in a semi-circle inside the perimeter, because in Yorkshire, no one, even a druid, likes sitting on ground, where they might get a wet bum.

The druids, who were more interested in the food aspect of things, had arrived with four large metal wheelbarrows heaped with all the equipment and supplies that a lover of barbecued food could ever need. Once they had unloaded, a metal grid with six feet was placed at the bottom of two barrows and capped by a large pierced ash pan ready for hot charcoal. Finally, with great ceremony, two large metal grids wide enough to overlap the edges of the wheelbarrows were placed reverently over their tops and fixed with metal crocodile clips to the galvanised steel edges.

Before the cooks could level up the legs on their extending camping tables and load the chimney starter with charcoal, they had a line of wild-looking men lining up in a panic in case they missed the first order for sausage, onion and bell pepper kebabs.

'Are you doing grilled tomatoes?'

'We are, Uther,' replied Cacklog the chef. 'Beef tomatoes from the vine, all from Pyrlig's greenhouse.' He wandered off to find his matches.

'OOOH, smashing! Got any bread buns?'

'I think we just brought pitta bread, Uther. Sorry, mate,' replied Cai, the youngest member of the catering team.

'Oh no. I don't like them, it's like eating ribbed cardboard with eczema. One of life's many unpleasantries. It almost ranks alongside *"mate"* as a default form of address for the young – when addressing the old,' he added caustically.

Cai wasn't quite sure if he'd been gently chastised or heavily insulted so he decided to look busy somewhere else.

'We brought some white baps too, Uther,' said Mary. 'There's four packs of twenty-four and a bread knife under the barrow on the tarp, Cai.'

'Oh, that's wonderful, Mary, I just can't hold my sausage properly unless it's between a firm pair of baps,' sighed Uther. 'I find pitta bread just crumbles all over your feet. Dreadful things… Could I have one bap, without onions – *I get terrible gas with onions,*' he mouthed silently. 'How much is it, dear?'

'Just a pound.'

'A pound?'

'Yes, love.'

'I'm sorry, my hearing's just not what it used to be.'

'Too many Zeppelin concerts?' enquired Mary with a smile.

'Yes! Absolutely. Two nights at Earl's Court in 1975. And then Motorhead at Hammersmith Odeon. More like terrorism, that was…I could probably sleep through World War Three with these ears…er, when will it be ready?'

'COME BACK WHEN WE BANG THE CYMBAL, UTHER!'

'Thank you, Mary.'

'MY PLEASURE.'

'Just one more question – are we getting two sausages in a bap?'

'YES, LOVE. TWO SAUSAGES IN A BAP.'

'Oh, that's splendid. I trust they're locally sourced?'

'ONLY THE BEST FOR THE PEOPLE OF THE TRUE RELIGION, UTHER.'

'I must say, you do know how to flatter a fellow, Mary. I'll shuffle off then – see you later. When you bang the cymbal?'

'YES, LOVE! COME BACK WHEN—'

'When you bang the cymbal.'

'I'll have two baps,' said the next chap in line. 'Plenty of onions, Mary.'

'Just one other thing, Mary,' asked Uther, squeezing back to the head of the line. 'Are you using lard, dear?'

'ONLY VEGETABLE OIL, UTHER.'

'AHHH, good. And is it margarine – on the bread?'

'Lurpak.'

'I suppose that'll be alright. Thank you, dear.'

'MY PLEASURE, UTHER.'

'We're just taking orders at the moment,' announced Mary to the growing crowd of anxious druids. 'Chef's just lighting the chimney starter to heat the charcoal properly before it goes in the grill on the barrow. IF YOU WANT SAUCE,' she yelled, 'WE GOT KETCHUP AND MUSTARD. Write your name and order on the tickets here and pass them to Cai.'

'OOOOH!'

'May the gods bless this feast!'

'There's some Heinz Salad Cream and HP Sauce in the box with the serviettes too, Mary, if anyone wants it,' added Cacklog.

'Have you got any balsamic vinegar?' asked the next fellow in line.

'No, pet. Ketchup, mustard sauce, salad cream or HP.'

'OH. Ermmm, have you got any veggie burgers?'

'Aye, we got a few packets o' them. Chef's just got to crack some eggs and mek 'em up.'

'They've got veggie burgers too!' went a call down the line.

'OOOOOOOH!'

'They've done us proud again.'

'CAN YOU MAKE TWO LINES, PEOPLE! ONE FOR SAUSAGES – AND ONE FOR BURGERS!' yelled Mary.

'Any chilli sauce, Mary?'

'We'll bring some up on Saturday, Menadith, if there's enough that want it. They'll be venison burgers tomorrow too and wild boar.'

'VENISON AND WILD BOAR ON SATURDAY, LADS! THREE CHEERS FOR CACKLOG AND MARY!'

As Derek and Maureen got nearer to their favourite conjuring location it became clear that it was far from empty of life. They could both see a large bonfire in the centre of the plateau where they always conducted their rituals and, rather alarmingly, a great many figures walking, standing and sitting in various places. Even more worryingly, there appeared to be an outdoor catering concession. And a potato oven. There were also many strange new piles of earth around the perimeter, and a circle of deep pits around the bonfire.

A family group was seated behind the bonfire on hay bales admiring the flames while others patrolled the fringes with flaming torches. Many of them appeared to be wearing long linen smocks to their ankles, wide leather belts and a variety of stout boots of the type common on building sites.

On the seaward side, a great oblong stone lay on a raft of tree trunks, next to a gigantic wooden 'A' frame fitted with metal pulleys. There were piles of ropes in various widths and colours, several reinforced nylon sacks full of hardcore and rubble on wheeled carts. A stack of wooden chocks, scaffolding planks and pit props lay on the ground to their front.

'Derek! There's lots of hairy men down there in funny nightshirts, with great big flaming torches.'

'DRUIDS! What the hell are they doing on our plateau!' fumed Derek. 'They've got their own damn groves and monuments on Landkey Island!'

'They've brought a great big rock with them. Are they trying to claim our plateau for themselves?'

'It certainly looks like it, doesn't it? It's not enough that every damn beauty spot in Great Britain's got one of their f***king great tombs in it – or some lichen-crusted stone circle.'

'Derek!'

'The lazy swines don't even bother smoothing their stones off, do they? Oh no! Far too much work for hairy old pagan has-beens! They just bang them up like wonky old teeth. No proper foundations. Then they fall over within a couple of hundred years and the next generations have to start all over again. Cowboy builders, the lot of 'em.'

'Your language is appalling, Derek Beautimann. You're just incensed because they're on our patch.'

'Aren't you!'

'I might have been, six months ago. As far as I'm concerned right at this moment they're welcome to it. I've had enough of the supernatural to last me two lifetimes. I want cake, *Coronation Street* and a warm cat on me lap from now on. I don't want any more indelible stains on my immortal soul, thank you very much. Anyway, our plateau's probably been ruined by all the pus and gunk that came out of that disgusting Tetarzepamdomestoz demon thing. Even the weeds haven't come back since that bloody thing exploded over the top of our heads – besides, it's not as if we can put up a sign that says "this picnic area is permanently reserved for the Black Hand Coven", can we?'

'We've got to get rid of this gold. Tonight!'

'I KNOW!'

'I can't believe our luck!' groaned Derek, squeezing his fists.

'Our luck ran out when you dug this up. I say we sneak past them and get on with it. Most of them look like they've had too much to drink to notice us anyway.'

'Well, there's no light falling on the original burial site, is there…? That fire is going to ruin their night vision.'

'Let's get going then, Derek. I'll help you bury it.'

'That's very generous, Maureen.'

'Don't expect me to keep up with you, I just want to get home quicker. Did the fire do much damage to your house?'

'It charred the far corner of the study, behind the filing cabinet. I lost my best squash racket. All our insurance paperwork. The files and records for both of our cars. The fire brigade said if they'd arrived two or three minutes later it would have been a lot worse. Sophie knows about the gold, Maureen.'

'WHAT! You didn't tell her about us, did you…? The coven, I mean.'

'Don't panic. I just explained we'd discovered it from my map and were going to declare it. Then I told her about the curse and how we were planning to re-bury it.'

'Well, I hope she keeps it a secret.'

'If she can't, she's not getting to keep the new MG she's forcing me to buy her.'

A roar of laughter cut through the night as two of the larger men began to 'belly bounce' each other around the fire.

'DAMN DRUIDS. WHO THE HELL DO THEY THINK THEY ARE!'

'SHUSH! They might hear you!'

'I've got a mind to go down there right now and set fire to their bloody rock crane and burn all their ropes!'

'What, just you on your own!'

'Why not!'

'Look at the size of them.'

'Bastards. THE LOT OF THEM. Dirty, smelly, rotten, stinking bastards!'

'Derek Beautimann, on my life, I've never heard you swear so much. Pull yourself together!'

'They'll pay for this. You mark my words…'

'You could always give them some of our cursed treasure. That'd fix 'em.'

'Maureen?'

'Yes, Derek?'

'This is one of those times when you really do earn your keep.'

On the opposite side of the druids' new circle at the edge of sight, Brian and David Drake stood in the shadows of the trees on the edge of the wood and observed the drunken merry-making.

'Druids in Cayton Bay!'

'They certainly seem to be druids, don't they…?A whole bloody clan of the buggers with their wives an' kids. This might make things tricky.'

'We could just dump it on the edge of the wood and scarper – just make a noise, let them take it.'

'We wouldn't even have to re-bury it, would we? Mmmm, I think on reflection we've made enough enemies, don't you?'

'Fair point – but we haven't got a spade,' grumbled Brian.

'AH, SHIT! I knew I had to bring something else. Damn it!…Hang on – we could shove it in one of those pits they've dug, on the dark side. Cover it up with a bit of soil, under that hay.'

'Where are you going to get a *bit of soil*?'

'I'll just kick some out the earth,' suggested Dave.

'*KICK SOME OUT OF THE EARTH? With what?*'

'Me foot… what else?'

'You could always use that Swiss army knife?'

Elsie Cakebread, a legend and icon for the local druids and the biker community, arrived on the queen seat of her husband's Honda Gold Wing to warm applause and raucous cheers.

The owners of Valhalla Retirement Home were the honoured guests of the druids for the weekend's celebrations, and two hay bales with blankets had been reserved especially for the Cakebreads. A large wooden cable reel, 'borrowed' for the evening from the engine shed at Seamer station, had been placed in front of their seats to serve as a table. It had been covered by two metres of weed control fabric stapled down to cover up the British Rail logo. Underneath the table was an old brittle cement bucket with a damp toilet roll in it. The druids of Whitborough on Sea were masters at spoiling their guests.

'This goes from bad to worse,' muttered Derek Beautimann, looking at the proceedings through a pair of binoculars.

'Who *is* that they're clapping?' asked Maureen.

'It's that bloody Cakebread woman, the owner of that Valhalla Retirement Home.'

'We went to her seance!'

'We certainly did. Never again!'

'Who's she with?'

'It looks like her husband.'

'Is that big oaf that was guarding her seance with them?'

'I can't see him, no.'

'I don't know what was worse. An evening with her or that bloody demon of ours Tetarzepamdomestoz.'

'It wasn't OUR demon, Maureen. But don't worry, it's not coming back. I took it to Sveta Anchabadze on Landkey Island to deal with.'

'Your fancy woman?'

'She's not my fancy woman.'

'You had a thing together. Didn't you ask her to sort out the others that came with this treasure?'

'No. Because once we've re-buried this cursed fortune, they'll leave us alone.'

'I bloody hope so.'

'I didn't like the sound of that one that came through at the seance. Even if that Cakebread woman did see it off.'

'She'd see anything off.'

'What was that other one called?'

'Quetzlcarbon Yum Taxx. It's a Mayan fire demon. Since I don't speak Mayan, we've been on a bit of sticky wicket.'

'Better get ourselves a fire extinguisher each if this doesn't go right.'

Chapter Four

As If by Magic, a Shopkeeper Appeared

Only once it was clear that the majority of the druids and their guests had reached peak inebriation did their uninvited visitors start to move. The bonfire still blazed brightly enough to make it relatively easy for them to get into position without revealing themselves, as long as they remained just beyond the reach of its light.

The Drake brothers had the easier task in theory, as their hole was already dug, but they still had to extend it enough to cover their remaining share of the treasure to cover a holdall the size of two of shoeboxes. Finding a spade in their chosen pit had certainly cheered them up and they were soon able to re-bury the coins and precious jewels that had been the cause of so much angst and misery. They had just thrown the hay back in to cover up their hard work and were brushing off some stray straw splinters when one of the druids tapped Brian on the shoulder.

'Hey, man! I know you… Clash Schiity Records – right? I shold you my ELO cleckshun, remember? Didn't know yous two wash one of ush, like. I'm Mordred,'he slurred, swaying slightly, transferring a can of McEwans to his left hand so he could extend his wavering right.

'Pleased to meet you,' replied Brian, quick as a flash,

pumping the hand of the wobbly druid. 'This is my brother Dave.'

'Delighted to meet you, Morbid,' said Dave.

'Itsh Morrdred.'

'Mordred.'

'Thas right, sorry – did you fall in our pit? I notished you was brushing off some straw. Fantashtic, int they?'

'Oh, yes!' agreed Brian. 'They're very well dug. Very neat.'

'No no, ELO, not them. Thems – pits. They're the pits. Where wash I going now…'

'*HE'S PISSED*,' mouthed Dave over the druid's shoulder.

'I know!' snapped the druid. 'I wash gonna get 'nother beer. You want a beer? We got lotsh han lotsh of beer.'

'Well, that'd be ni—'

'Very kind of you, mate, but we've got to be going,' said Brian, cutting off his younger brother.

'Well, it wash good to see y'here. Good of yous to come. Did you get rid of it all?'

The two brothers stared tensely at each other for a moment. Then Dave decided to call his bluff. 'What did we get rid of, Mordred?'

'Me records – of course,' he said, with a slightly confused look.

'OH! We sold most of them quite quickly. Didn't we, Dave?' said Brian, with a huge sigh of relief.

'We did, Brian.'

'Good. Anyways, I musht be getting back to shome where,' muttered Mordred, looking left and right. 'Over there I was somewhere… I'll call in shee you shoon… fellas… at your sh-shop.'

'Goodnight then, Mordred,' said Dave.

'Night, mate,' said Dave, before he and his brother jogged away into the dark.

Mordred walked on a few yards in the darkness then stopped again to look about, in an attempt to get his bearings. Finding the bonfire was now behind him, he turned around and began to stumble back to his party and then fell headfirst into the next pit.

'Did you hear that, Derek?' asked Maureen.

'Sorry?'

'I thought I heard somebody cry out nearby.'

'Don't interrupt me unless someone gets close to us, woman,' hissed Derek. 'This digging's hard enough on me without the benefit of your speculative commentary. If you heard somebody cry out, it was probably just one of those drunken oafs falling into one of their pits.'

'I was trying to get a conversation out of you. That's all. I'll just shut up then, shall I?'

'Will you please just watch my back while I'm digging? I can't talk *AND* dig. I'm a long time past my prime.'

'Suit yourself.'

Chapter Five

Speed Demon

Tapas Molinos, the Spanish half of the demon dream team protecting the Treasure of the Mar del Norte, had been very busy building up his strength on the lower planes of Hell, since his awkward humiliation at the hands of Elsie Cakebread.

He'd managed to collect just enough psychic energy for a few minutes' manifestation in Whitborough on Sea on his new 'horse', a brutal Kawasaki 750 two-stroke triple built by Elsie's spirit guide 'Robert 'Roll-up' Benson. The deceased former workshop mechanic at Kawasaki Scarborough, whose new life as a ghost was far less painful than the exit from his earthbound life, pinned and crushed on a drip tray underneath the Cakebread's enormous Honda Gold Wing. There were far fewer hazards in the astral world, though sleep, lunch breaks and paid holidays – any sort of holidays – were now completely out of the question.

Tapas Molinos was delighted with his new ride. It was just the thing for a demon who wanted to make waves in the modern world. The giant two-stroke Kawasaki was ear-splittingly loud, insanely fast and left impressively foul clouds of toxic petrochemical smog behind him wherever he went. Nothing in Hell's equine stables could ever hope to compete with it, including the red-eyed black stallions usually favoured by Spanish demons. With hoops of flaming napalm and sulphur, in place of the skinny Japanese tyres and spoke wheels, it was as close to perfection as anything he could ever mount in Hell.

It was just the kind of evil machine he hoped would scare the pants off the pathetic human thieves who had taken the treasure he was committed to guard after the Spanish Armada took an unexpected detour around the British Isles.

The druids' barbecue was going to be his last chance to show off in the physical world, before the treasure was re-interred, and so he selected a nice long stretch of road to pick up some speed before he attempted the leap from the end of Higher Gunstone, over the canopy of Kenwith Woods and onto the plateau. A long jump, even if you were a demon astride a two-stroke shooting star.

Inspector Marshall and Detective Sergeant Broadhead arrived in their unmarked car outside Cayton Boat Builders yard at the furthest end of Higher Gunstone, just as Tapas Molinos began his run from Cornelian Drive. They had just stepped out of Marshall's Vauxhall Cavalier and were buttoning up their macs when they heard the distant wail of a large motorcycle gobbling tarmac at full throttle.

'Now what?' grumbled Broadhead, glancing down the road. 'Another hooligan going for gold.'

'Let's wait until the bloody fool goes past, George, he might be someone we know.'

Tapas Molinos had got the tuned Kawasaki howling in third through its shiny new expansion chambers and firmly in the lift-off zone of its deadly power band. He changed up into fourth gear, maintaining the eye-melting acceleration – then suddenly, his front wheel began to spit tiny pips of napalm back at him. Something else was wrong too: the handlebars had started to shake – and it was getting worse. He gritted his teeth and changed up into fifth, hoping a higher gear and more revs might calm things down. As he crested the second-to-last rise before the boat yard the subtle weight transfer to the back wheel caused the slow shake of the front to switch into a full-on tank-slapper once the front re-connected with terra firma. Tapas Molinos panicked and stamped on the back brake pedal, only to remember too late that because he had given in to vanity and wheels of fire, he had no longer had any brakes and his throttle had stuck.

On the safe side of the last crest, the two policemen scurried back behind the safety of their Vauxhall and instinctively ducked down as the flaming bike blasted over their heads, gaining height before smashing through the upper branches of the trees above Kenwith woods. Seconds later there was dull crump followed by a huge bang and a great donut-shaped ball of frame in a (carbon) copy of a nuclear explosion shot up into the sky.

'Holy Mary, Mother of God,' whispered Inspector Marshall.

Some of the druids who were facing in the direction of the immolation began to whistle and cheer. But not all of their companions, especially their elder members, were quite so happy with the extra entertainment.

'I don't see why we're having fireworks *and* a barbecue tonight. It's all a little too modern for my tastes. We should stick to the old ways. Not try to turn every ceremony into a circus,' grumbled Belator to Pyrlig as the sub-sonic headstock and upper fork stanchions of the Kawasaki streaked overheard, slicing a rotting sycamore tree in half in the darkness.

Mordred, who had managed to struggle back up to the lip of his foundation pit, lost his grip and found himself back in the bottom when a napalm-spotted mudguard crashed down onto the edge of the pit beside him. He watched it burn what was left of the turf for a few minutes, trying to think where it might have come from, but he soon gave up contemplating fiery foreign objects and struggled back out of his hole, zig-zagging back to the beer crates like a sagging marathon runner.

Derek and Maureen had also stopped momentarily to watch the pyrotechnics then resumed their work scattering loose bark and wet leaves over their excavations, double-checking the ground to be sure there was nothing to indicate there had been yet another burial.

'What do you suppose that great big bang was over there, Derek?' asked Maureen quietly.

'Something, I fear, that was probably intended for us, bearing in mind all the trouble this has brought. So much better for us that it's fallen short,' replied Derek, standing up to inspect the ground. 'A successful night's work considering the circumstances,' he sighed. 'Time to take a wide circle back to your car, Maureen.'

'Maybe it was a gas bottle.'

'I haven't the faintest idea. Now the source of our discontent is back in its grave perhaps our fortunes will start to improve.'

'Weren't we going to hold a bit back and give it to the druids?'

'I forgot,' mumbled Derek wearily. 'What does it matter anyway…? I'm exhausted. Let's go home.'

Chapter Six

No Doubt About It

Cai, the youngest member of the Whitborough Brotherhood of Bards and Druids – Cacklog's apprentice grill man – decided to take his two cans of stolen cider into the woods to steady his nerves as he set off to find out if the enormous fireball at the top of Kenwith Wood had actually been caused by a UFO crash. As a lover of sci-fi and a fan of all things extra-terrestrial he had all but convinced himself that he was on the verge of discovering a Yorkshire Roswell.

In a camp full of men obsessed with signs and omens, the young druid was a little puzzled that he appeared to be the only one interested in finding out what had caused the spectacular explosion, until he saw the bin of empty mead, ale and scrumpy containers; so he set off on his own – the last man standing, full of expectations and dreams with his flapjack, his little torch and a roll of fluorescent tape to mark out prominent branches on his way up, so that when he got there, he could actually find his way back without ending up in hospital for his pains.

Cai also purloined a handful of heavy-duty bin liners and a Booth's Supermarket 'bag for life', just in case there were any valuable grey alien body parts scattered about or interesting chunks of UFO flight deck. If there was any physical evidence of alien technology, he certainly wasn't going to leave it to the foxes and badgers.

The point of impact was a shallow depression in front of a fallen tree, filled with bluebells and mushrooms. After the crash, the pretty woodland scene had taken on the appearance of a half-finished World War One dugout that had been shelled before it had even seen a duckboard. What wasn't black and crisp was hissing or smoking under the orange spittle of napalm and a burning gravy of petrol and Castrol R. The bike that had given Roll-up so much pride was now so twisted and buckled that it hardly resembled a motorcycle at all.

There were still flames aplenty when Cai reached it. He didn't really need his torch because the smell alone had been enough to find it.

Tapas Molinos, the pilot of the crashed UFO, was long gone and in intensive care in Demon Hospital. He had months of painful regeneration ahead of him, a long wait for a pair of donor arms and legs and a difficult 'fitness to practice' interview with Hell's most unpleasant accident investigation committee.

Quetzlcarbon Yum Taxx, the Mayan half of the treasure's protection team, was not best pleased with his impulsive Spanish compatriot's demise. Their shared conservatorship had never been a match made in hell but one made by humans. He was going to have to manage on his own.

Now the bulk of The Treasure was back in its grave. He could strike out much of the work on his revenge list. There were just two coins now left in circulation, in English hands. One was taped inside a black Doc Marten boot at the BADCOW punk commune in Burniston Village and the other was in the bottom of a Belfast sink in one of the outbuildings on the Charlwood Estate of Sir William Henry Warner Woollens, waiting to have its sooty face scrubbed.

Yum Taxx might have already added Charlwood Hall to his CV of destruction had the bureau in which the coin in question was resting not been so airtight. Instead of a country-house blaze to remember, all he had made was a desk full of soot.

Before he got back into the revenge business, there was one remaining duty to perform in Kenwith Woods for his former colleague Tapas Molinos. A short physical manifestation in the treetops above the crash, in recognition of their long service together. Yum Taxx elected to manifest in his shimmering Mayan sky warrior outfit; with the enclosed helmet and chunky block armour, it was just the right amount of bling to send off an old friend.

On the ground below, Cai couldn't quite decide where to stand or what to look at. He found an old branch free of leaves and began to prod about in the crater, but as soon as it touched one of the hot orange blobs the tip burst into flames. He guessed that the little puddles of orange gel must be the contents of extra-terrestrial fuel cells. He dropped the branch, just in case it was warp-strength nuclear anti-matter.

Searching further out, he began to see that there were many fragments of what seemed to be the frame of its hull structure, covered in a mirror-like metal finish and shards of a light orange and red material resembling plastic with a reflective quality to them. He could hardly contain his mounting excitement but puzzlingly there was very little evidence remaining of what he guessed had once been a massive ship.

He decided to sit down on a rock nearby and drink the cider to calm his nerves until the crash site had cooled down sufficiently for him to probe deeper for relics or possible skeletons. Just in time to witness Quetzlcarbon Yum Taxx teleporting in from another dimension as an 'ancient alien'.

It was the noise that made him look up. Like a jet turbine starting up beside a giant vacuum cleaner. The upper branches of the trees above him were being pulled towards a rotating black void wreathed in lightning. Then his ears popped and a humanoid figure in a golden armoured astronaut suit appeared, after a painfully bright flash, hovering over the crash site. It pointed a golden rod at the crater, firing a plasma bolt at the ground. Then the figure folded its arms and disappeared.

Cai felt for the second can of Strongbow. Never before in his life had he ever needed a drink like now. Trembling with wonder – and fright – he managed to get the ring pull off and bump the can against his bottom lip, getting it plumb on his second attempt. He didn't need to open his mouth. It was already as wide open as it had ever been.

Chapter Seven

Very Superstitious

'I don't suppose there's any point in making more enquiries tonight, George,' sighed Inspector Marshall as his eyes wandered back to the gap in the treetops made by the flying Kawasaki. 'We'll come back at six in the morning, when that lot below are still in their sleeping bags, have a good sniff around Evel Knievel's crater and then go and talk to our new friends the druids on the green before they start on that bloody great slab of rock. I hope they remembered to untie the old bugger they'd strapped on to it.'

'That bike was really was flying, wasn't it? It was *actually* flying, Ray.'

'Think about what you're saying, George.'

'You saw it too.'

'I may well have done, but don't make the mistake of thinking you're going to improve your prospects in life by telling other people at the station about it. We don't have a big fan club at work at the moment.'

'I suppose you're right. But it's going to be a tough ask writing this case up without mentioning stuff like this.'

'All I'm trying to do is make sure it's us that writes it up. That means we have to leave out stuff like this. You haven't told anyone about the werewolf getting blown away in front of our eyes in Cloughton, have you?'

'No, I certainly haven't.'

'We're going to go leave now – and we're not going to mention this to anybody ever again. It's the only way to deal these things. Let's just try and type up the things that aren't going to get us in the more downmarket gossip magazines as paranormal investigators. Or our careers are going to go up in flames like that bloody idiot on the flying motorbike. Fancy a curry?'

'What a good idea. It's been nearly three weeks. I could do with a Castella afterwards as well, Ray.'

'I'm well stocked up in that department, George.'

Chapter Eight

Rock On

Sunrise after the first night of the druids' celebrations brought clear blue skies once the mist that often clung to the plateau above Cayton Bay began to evaporate. The druids began to stir in their tents, caravans and motor homes, getting ready for the business of the day. Cacklog and Mary switched on their generator and potato oven, and soon a fresh batch of charcoal was tipped into the chimney starter for the barbecue barrows. They connected the twin two-burner gas hob to the gas bottle, raised another portable table, chalked up the blackboard, and soon the kitchen that had served so many head-bangers for so many years at the Monsters of Rock festival was operational once again. They were a little puzzled by Cai, who seemed to be overly cheerful one minute and then brooding on some great secret the next.

'You alright, lad?'

'I'm fine.'

'You been taking something we should know about?'

'I've only had two cans of cider, Dad.'

'Mystery solved, Mary. The boy's owned up!'

'I'll pay for 'em.'

'Oh, I know you will. Did you nick some of the bin liners and me "bag for life" too?'

'Yeah. I was litter picking near the wood, though.'

'Well, good for you. Now go and help your mother prep them baked tatties. Derrigans Butchers are bringing down our order of venison and wild boar steaks around noon – if me or your mum are busy, make sure the count in the boxes tallies with the invoice. They're not cheap, these steaks. We gonna have a very busy day today. You get enough sleep last night?'

'Er, yeah.'

Very quickly, the big chrome tea urns were primed and connected to their own extension cables and thence to the generator, and a table was cleared for paper plates, cups, napkins and cutlery.

Druids never did anything physical in the modern age before at least two cups of tea and a full cooked breakfast. It was a time for summoning strength, for burping, a time for high fives, greasy double handshakes, teeth-rattling back slaps and weight-lifting belts.

Once the scaffolding and lifting teams had breakfasted, they were both summoned into the company of Pyrlig, the vertically challenged senior druid who had brought his own little dais, topped with a Welsh slate plinth, so that he could crack the bottom of his staff if he saw anybody's attention wandering. Pyrlig assigned each man his role and then talked through the sequence of tasks required to elevate the first and largest stone. Meanwhile, their sons ferried the frame sections, pulleys and scaffolding boards to their assembly areas. Three families of log pit props in ascending lengths followed four groups of ropes of varying thicknesses to a reserved space beside the central foundation pit, and the first log roller sequence was laid down before the stone.

Down on the plateau, the proceedings had attracted a good turnout from curious members of the public and a journalist and photographer from the *Whitborough Evening News*.

Inspector Marshall and Detective Sergeant Broadhead were sniffing about for any titbits of information concerning the Black Hand Coven's recent on-site activities at the plateau, but nothing was forthcoming from the druids, who considered the matter irrelevant and rather beneath them. Derek and Maureen had also arrived, but only Maureen had left their car. Derek had elected to conceal himself behind an AA road atlas to avoid being recognised whilst Maureen checked that no one had disturbed their new excavations.

Maureen found that she was actually enjoying watching the men set up; they were the kind of heavyweight masculine alpha males that she'd always admired from afar. Observing their preparations was almost as arousing as watching a professional rugby team – in beards. Very nearly all of them were as large and beefy as the prop forwards and door-wrecking flankers of so many not-so-secret female fantasies. They obviously enjoyed their food, just as she always had, although she now felt a little ashamed she was not doing quite as much as the men she was admiring to manage her circumference.

No one could ever have accused her of being lazy as such, because she had always been such a dedicated scrubber at home, never shirking her domestic chores, the vacuuming, the polishing, the plumping – the washing and ironing performed with a determination and frequency that had brought poor Bert, her Parsons terrier, to the brink of a nervous breakdown. Her poor dog's nose had endured more of ICI and Proctor and Gamble's chemical preparations than the carpets and soft furnishings of a small hotel. He had only managed to save himself by pushing his head into her laundry basket of bed socks and novelty pyjama sets every time she had the urge.

Cleaning had been the only serious form of exercise Maureen had ever persevered with. But every time she had finished, she'd ruin all her hard work by eating two chocolate eclairs and a Flake – and so she was as plush as one of her cushions. All the wine she was getting through wasn't helping her waistline either.

Maureen was torn between two contradictory desires. A desire to be seen – but not seen in any way in which she could be looked up and down. Especially in the unflattering dimensions of width and depth. Gripped by the kind of desperation that only a plump, plain deputy witch on heat could churn up, she looked about for something that might hide the bulk of her outline from serious male scrutiny, whilst giving herself a clear field of view. The best thing she could find was a tripod, holding a large map case and a Barbour coat. With all the cunning and subterfuge learnt on her long road to the menopause, she tucked in between the tripod and the bushes, and had just got comfortable when the druid directing proceedings stepped off his plinth and started striding towards her with his minder Belator – almost a menhir himself.

'Get away from the level!' yelled Pyrlig.

'OH, SORRY!' replied Maureen, mortified at being singled out for a tongue-lashing in front of the crowd.

'*Don't touch that level*,' he shouted, waving his arms. '*Go away!*'

'I'm going – I'm going!' she pleaded, backing away from the tripod. 'SORRY!'

Belator, Pyrlig's understudy and rival for the most frightening druid in Northern England, gave Maureen a look that could not be misinterpreted as anything but a death threat by facial expression.

'That's that legal secretary from Beautimann Buerk and Trippe, is it not, Belator?' asked Pyrlig, grinding his teeth.

'Coven people,' replied Belator, launching a vindictive bullet of spit onto the grass.

'*Fix them*, Belator. Not the witches. I have plans for them.'

'Their master waits in her car, shall I make sure he leaves?'

'No. I need you here. Send Lod. Tell Lod to follow him – and if he leaves their car, if he goes anywhere near our equipment, take him for a chat… above the cliffs.'

'A chat?'

'Yes. One of those chats that you don't come back from.'

Chapter Nine

The Road to Hell, Is Paved with Cake

Derek had finally run out of patience waiting for Maureen to report back and realised he was going to have to leave her car to find his missing driver. He pulled up his collar, pulled down the peak of his hat and strode into the crowd, trying to keep his eyes near the grass to avoid any unnecessary eye contact. He had seen Inspector Marshall and his antagonistic partner milling about and was determined to avoid a conversation at all costs. Marshall had a witness who had identified him as the Master of Ceremonies for the Black Hand Coven on the night when their ritual had ended in disaster. He didn't want to be seen anywhere near the scene of the crime twice. Eventually he found her beside the caterers' end table in the shadow of one of the tea urns.

'So this is where you've been!' hissed Derek, taking his deputy by surprise.

'Derek! You scared the life out of me.'

'What are you doing?'

'I'm… I'm observing.'

'You're oggling those druids.'

'What if I am?'

'What you do in your own time is your own business. When you're working for me, I expect you to do those things I require of you and then inform me without delay.'

'Sorry. I just lost track of myself.'

'Did you notice if our excavation had been disturbed?'

'It looks fine.'

'Good. Here are your car keys. I'll make my own way home.'

'Are you sure, Derek?'

'Very sure. You might want to hide behind something bigger than that urn.'

'Do you mind!'

'The police are here.'

'*Oh, bloody hell!*'

'Oh, bloody hell indeed.'

'Inspector Marshall and his equally delightful detective sergeant.'

'I'll go back with you.'

'I'm not going to risk it. I'm going to walk home past the holiday camp.'

'OH. All the way back that way?'

'Yes. It's not that far. May I suggest it's probably best if we split up? Go back to your car along the edge of the wood. You should be alright. Just pretend to be out walking. They probably don't remember you anyway.'

'But they've seen me in your chambers.'

'Very briefly. In different clothes.'

'You want me to walk all the way round the back?'

'It's your only option if you don't want to take the chance, unless you're going to wait until they're gone. Did you know your friends are here too?'

'I'm not built for long walks!'

'That's hardly my fault, is it, Maureen? Might I suggest you cut back on the cake and lose some weight? Then you might even be able to bag yourself a druid. A very short-sighted one.'

'Cheeky swine!'

'Your lady friends are here,' added Derek.

'I know. I'm trying to hide so they don't call out to me...'

Violet Penrose, Joy Blanchard and Phyllis Elliott arrived in their heels, minis and full war-paint just in time to steal the best vantage point for the biggest erection of stone since Whitborough Castle was started. Being the cunning, manipulative ladies of sin they were, the three witches had detailed two of their strongest nephews to carry their folding chairs, tables and picnic basket so they could arrive with the least amount of effort. Once the two young men had placed the camping furniture to their satisfaction and the heavy picnic basket was opened it became clear why it had clinked so loudly. Apart from two packets of Tunnock's tea cakes and a Black Forest gateau, it was full of gin, vodka, Bacardi, whisky and sparkling wine. The ladies were obviously there to make a day of it.

Also making a day of it were the members of the East Yorkshire Ancient Warrior Society, who were doing a shield wall re-enactment and an afternoon of single combat demonstrations as guests of the druids. But they had already been warned by their high council that anyone coming dressed as a Saxon wouldn't be able to buy a ticket for the barbecue or use the toilets.

Michael, the assistant manager at Clash City Records, had been gifted a second-hand Ford 2.8i Capri by his employers the Drake brothers as compensation for retrieving their gold from the zoo. It was just the thing for transporting his girlfriend Fenella and her sword, Skull Splitter, to Cayton Bay. They had even managed to squeeze her friend Desira in behind but found they had to wind down the front passenger window to get her pole-axe in. It had been a test to squeeze their willow board shields and first aid bag in the boot, but eventually the boot catch clicked and the two young lady warriors and their chauffeur sped off.

'It's got a big bonnet, this thing,' said Desira from the back. 'What's it like to drive, Mike?'

'It's got a bit too much power for the brakes and the chassis, but it should be pretty good fun on a runway or an empty dual carriageway, Desira.'

'Well, I like it. Even squeezed in back here. It's got balls. And it looks great in black. Are you keeping your Triton?'

'Oh, aye! I'm not getting rid of that.'

'Dave and Brian bought Amie a big Land Rover Desira,' added Fenella. 'I wondered what she did to get that, apart from having her Mini burnt to a crisp, of course.'

'She's got something on Dave and Brian, I think. Something sharp and deadly probably,' said Michael with a smirk. 'Talking of sharp and deadly, have you got the St John's Ambulance there today as usual?'

'They're parking their ambulance as close as they can, in the bottom corner of the holiday camp near the end of the path so they can get any casualties out quick.'

'So the ambulance crew are just going down with their bags and a stretcher?'

'Yep.'

'Well, have a good battle, girls. Hope it doesn't turn into a finger buffet…'

Chapter Ten

Get It On

'Make your line's taut before you lean into it,' shouted Pyrlig through his megaphone. 'Be smooth and don't snatch at the ropes, watch the fellow on your opposite side and keep yourselves parallel – the marshals will keep you on a straight heading, so listen to them and adjust yourselves as necessary. Don't go faster than the forward log-placing team can work. *Jolly good then… off you go!*'

The crowd applauded as the druids stamped their boots into the earth and took the strain. The complete absence of grass and weeds in the centre of the site was going to make the erection significantly easier. No one had thought to ask why it was so clear. The druids thought their gods had cleared it for them as a sign that they wanted a new henge. The few members of the Black Hand Coven who had turned up to watch knew otherwise.

Would the old gods wipe out the last traces of one of Satan's most poisonous ambassadors? The thousands of gallons of intravenous fluids belonging to Tetarzepamdomestoz, Hell's Minister of Mines, Caves and Underground Car Parks, could only kill grass for so long. But even his bodily fluids weren't as dangerous to life as Violet and Joy's idea of blended spirits.

'Look at those fellas with the logs, Vi,' purred Joy. 'OOOOH, rapture!'

'You two have got 'em all undressed already,' muttered Phyllis under her breath.

'That's what we're here for,' replied Violet.

'So's Maureen over yonder. Trying to hide her big arse. I could have sworn I saw Derek with her. They're up to something, those two,' added Phyllis. 'I wonder why she's not come over to say hello.'

'She's hiding from somebody. She probably thinks we'll blow her cover – and he's scarpered.'

'She's had a telling-off…'

'Never mind them, look, the fellas are just about there. The shirts are coming off, girls!'

'EEEE, all this excitement's giving me the munchies. I fancy a tea cake. Anybody else?'

'Hot bods and chocolate, it's a grand day out, girls!'

'We've got the East Yorkshire Ancient Warrior Society smashing the hell out of each other later on. Might be worth a look,' said Joy.

'Arthur and the Britons!' cackled Violet, remembering the 1970s HTV series based on the legend of King Arthur. '*Oliver Tobias!* Oooh, blimey, he were lush, weren't he? Drop-dead bloody gorgeous.' She sighed.

'David Essex!' cooed Joy.

'He wasn't in that,' replied Violet.

'He was in Jackie. An' everything else.'

'I wish he'd been in me,' mumbled Phyllis.

'You randy cow!'

'I'd have to get up pretty early to beat you, Violet Penrose,' countered Phyllis.

'And go to bed a hell of a lot later.' Joy grinned.

'You're just jealous, girls,' replied Violet haughtily. 'Pass us another tea cake…'

Chapter Eleven

You Ain't Nothin' But a Hound Dog

Dudley Kingcombe, Devon's most proficient big cat killer, sat uneasily in the waiting room of Aveyou Nympton's only doctors' surgery trying his best to look relaxed and carefree, but he was failing miserably to conceal a restlessness of posture that was making his waiting-room companions more than a little concerned.

However much he tried he just couldn't get himself comfortable on his chair. It was almost as if something demonic had got into his bloodstream and his head – and was taking him over from the inside.

In the space of a minute he'd scratched his chest, the back of his neck, then caught himself scratching his ear, sending his leg into a sympathetic canine-like spasm. The gentleman bedside him had suddenly developed an acute lean away towards the wall that indicated he was just one more scratch from getting up and moving to another seat.

Dudley tried to stop fidgeting by attempting to analyse the small paintings of rural life along the walls, to focus on something else and avoid eye contact with his fellow sitters. But he just couldn't keep his eyes drifting to the floor where his nose had picked up the fading scent of a cat; he tried a magazine but quickly swiftly replaced it when he'd felt an overwhelming urge to sniff the pages.

Finally, the gentleman beside him stood up and walked to the reception desk, taking the longest route around the coffee table to avoid having to move in front of him. He leant forward and whispered something to the receptionist, then walked briskly and purposefully out of the surgery in a huff and into the car park.

Dudley, to his surprise, heard every word of their whispered exchange and couldn't stop himself standing up to address the last three occupants and the lady at reception to put a stop to any more talk of fleas, scabies or eczema.

'Jus' ta clear up a foo misconceptions, folks, oi ain't got fleas, oi don't 'ave scabies an' oim perdy sure it ain't the Black Death that's givin' me aggravation, are we clear on that? Roight. An' I don't 'ave contagious hay fever oither.'

'That's lovely to hear, young man,' said the very elderly lady opposite. 'You really don't need to explain.'

'Very noice of eee ta say so, maam,' replied Dudley. 'Oi jus' had to say sumthen', see. Can't 'ave every bugger, sorry… can't 'ave every stranger calling me a fleabag. It ain't roight.'

'Yes, of course. I do sympathise with you,' she said testily. 'I can see that you seem to be a little out of sorts. Would you like to go in before me…? I'm not in a hurry.'

'Dudley, maaam.'

'You go in before me then, Dudley.'

'And me,' said the other man. 'I'm not in any hurry either,' he added weakly, coughing to cover up a slight quaver in his speech, then he smiled rather tautly, crossed his legs and moved ever so slightly further away from Dudley's chair.

At last, the receptionist called on Dudley to walk down to Dr Whittle's office and then everyone present breathed a sigh of relief as they watched the bow-legged former sniper amble down the short corridor into the doctor's consulting room.

Dudley was praying his restlessness had been caused by spending too long hunting and tracking out of doors. Mainly because he couldn't bear to think about the alternative. Being forced to hunt two werewolves in the space of a month, despite the generous expenses and open brief, seemed to be turning into the adventure of a lifetime. He was a little worried that he was actually starting to enjoy getting in close to his victims. Using the Mossberg special forces shotgun was a deceptively satisfying experience, especially with the solid one-ounce shot. It was the kind of combination that worked like an anti-aircraft gun; there was no skill or subtlety in its operation, but it always left such incredibly fascinating scenes of carnage. It was as satisfying as using artillery at point-blank range. On the plus side, he was also saving time cleaning up afterwards. The things he had shot with it had almost disappeared.

Hunting supernatural creatures in Yorkshire meant he was at least free of Ella Furnish, who was very nearly as unpleasant a prospect as the werewolves. She was a lady who could have been the Fran Cotton of women's rugby, if only she'd not found so much enjoyment bullying livestock and husbands.

His parents had clung to the fantasy that she was the only answer to the impending gap in their family tree. Well-meaning as they were, on this particular topic they were as far away from their son in terms of his wishes as they had ever been on any subject. Dudley had other ideas, which didn't include suicide by matrimony. The only thing he had ever wanted to press against Ella Furnish was the tip of a 240-volt stun lance.

'What can I do for you, Mr Kingcombe?'

'Well, Doc, I just wann – ned to ask eee if there's such a thing as the male menopatch.'

The doctor looked puzzled for a second but then realised what Dudley had meant to say, deciding to wait for a polite interval before correcting his patient.

'If such a condition exists, Mr Kingcombe, I'm sure medical science will reveal it in time. At the moment, I think we can safely discount the possibility.'

'That's a no then, is it?'

'It's a no.'

'Roight…'

'Is there anything in particular that you wanted to talk to me about? Any performance issues in the bedroom?'

'What?' replied Dudley, looking completely lost.

'Is your problem about sex?'

'EH?'

'You said you had a personal problem when you called to make your appointment, Mr Kingcombe, and you didn't want to divulge any details. Is there an issue with your sex life, Mr Kingcombe?'

'NO, THERE BLEDDY AIN'T. *An' if ever there t'was you wouldn't be 'earing about it frum me!* What oi got, what oi came yerr to see eee about, ain't nothen' to do with a sex loife. Oi jus' drove four 'undred miles from Honiton, to get away from a sex loife. An' if you'd ever saw 'er yerself you'd know why. Ain't nothing to do with sex. It's about me glands… at least oi think it's about me glands.'

'My apologies, Mr Kingcombe, I assumed from your first comment you were alluding to problems of a sexual nature. Most men find do find impotence an incredibly difficult and touchy subject to talk about.'

'If you'd seen the maid moi parents got in store for me back 'ome,' chuckled Dudley, 'then you'd get impotent faster than you can fall out a tree. If you could call 'er a maid. 'Er looks more loike she wuz "maid" in one o' they East German tank factories.'

The doctor's next glance was the full equivalent of the comment that had almost got out through the doors of his lips. He swallowed it with the least amount of effort and continued with a new caution. 'What are your physical symptoms, Mr Kingcombe?'

'Well, oim not feverish, not been sick as such. Fact is, Doc, bits of me suddenly got better, my hearing got so good oi can hear a mouse fart at t'other end of a barn. I can smell a cold kebab, in a bin at the t'other soide o' the village. An' oi swear oi can see things in the dark oi never could afore, like oi suddenly got night-vision implants in me eyeballs. Ain't all good tho'. Oive got hairs growing where I never had hairs growing before too. An' every toime oi pass a bleddy lamp post or a gate oi gets this urge...'

'Urge?'

'To cock me bleddy leg.'

'You've got an urge to cock your leg?' asked the doctor feeling his day sliding to a new doom.

'Gates, bins. Trees. Bus stops, bushes. Oi daren't go out on bin day!'

'You're normally continent, are you?'

'Content as the next man.'

'No, continent, Mr Kingcombe.'

'Sorry?'

'I'm just trying to get to the bottom of things.'

'Me backside is fine, just in case you were gonna ask…
'replied Dudley without much warmth. 'Oim reglurr as the
next man.'

The doctor took a deep breath and gently cleared his
throat. His consultation was not going quite how he'd
imagined it should, but he reminded himself that he'd
had many difficult and occasionally risky doctor/patient
interactions over the years. Sliding his chair forwards on
its castors, he found his 'Doctor requires assistance' button
underneath his desk with his knee but decided against using
it for the moment.

'Have you ever used drugs, Mr Kingcombe?'

'Drugs?'asked Dudley guardedly. 'What do eee mean…
paracetamol, Horlicks, stuff like that?'

'LSD, marajuana, opoids?'

'No, oi bloody 'aven't. What's an opoid?'

'I believe you, Mr Kingcombe. I just have to ask.'

'Oid never take any o' that rubbish. Oim a working man.
Not a bleddy student. Are you gonna take a blood sample off
me then or what?'

'I may do if that's required.'

'Fair enough. It's still no.'

'A no?'

'Drugs.'

'Very good. Now, you say you've grown hairs where you
never had them before? Do you have more hair in your ears
and your nose?'

'Oi do, Doc, funny you should ask that.'

'That's perfectly normal at your age.'

'I gots a great new patch of hair down the middle of me shoulder blades an' all. Is that normal?'

'Well, that's not so unusual in middle age.'

'On me palms?'

'*In your palms?*'

'An' on the bottom of me feet too.'

'*The bottom of your feet?*'

'Oive had to start shaving it off me palms every morning. It's a bit embarrassing, see, but there's the stubble look… in the middle. Plain as day,' he said, presenting the doctor with both his palms. Neither Dudley nor the Doctor spoke, but there was no doubt about it. There were two distinct areas of stubble in the centre of both of his hands.

'Oh my goodness. That is *odd*.'

'Told you oi wasn't joken'.'

The doctor paused for a moment, took down a medical reference book and skimmed through a list of rare skin conditions, talking to Dudley as he looked for an old case he had remembered from medical school.

'I seem to remember a case from my days in medical school, it has been a few years now…Do you recall seeing those famous photographs of the hairy man and the bearded lady promoted by a famous circus in the Victorian era? They were very rare conditions. I'm afraid we are still as puzzled by conditions like these in the modern era as much as we were all those years ago, Mr Kingcombe.'

'You're the man, Doc.'

'Would you mind if I took a look in your ears?'

'Be my guest, can't say there's ever been much wrong

with 'em.'

'Could you lie down on the bench for me, Mr Kingcombe? Just relax and lean back on the head rest so I can do an ear examination.'

'Okay, Doc.'

Doctor Whittle stood up and drew out the height-adjustable examination stool from under his desk, pushing it around to Dudley's right side on its castors then adjusted the seat so his sight line was level with Dudley's ear canal, then took out his Otoscope from his mobile instrument cabinet.

'Just relax, Mr Kingcombe.'

'Help yourself, Doc.'

The doctor took out a clean plastic comb, parted the hair above Dudley's ear and suddenly went very still. Dudley heard him swallow hard then cough to the side. It seemed as though he was suddenly lost for something to say or concentrating very hard.

'Everything ship-shape, Doc? I cleans 'em out with buds, offen as oi can. Ears loike little round shells we got. Uzz Kingcombes. Doc?'

'I have to go the front desk for a moment.'

'Do eee want me to stay yerr?'

'Umm… yes.'

A few minutes passed and Dudley remained alone, he turned his head when he caught sight of another doctor hurrying past the fire door's glass panel and a figure that seemed to be from reception dashing in the opposite direction. More time passed and still he remained alone. Feeling restless, he swung his legs off the couch and sat up. For no particular reason he picked up a hand mirror and walked over to the larger mirror on the wall behind the door, holding up the hand mirror so he could see his ear.

'WELL, BUGGER ME!'

'You want me to go and tell Mr Kingcombe that you had to leave to attend an emergency,' repeated the receptionist to Doctor Whittle.

'Yes.'

'But you're not actually leaving…and we don't have an emergency?'

'Correct.'

'Where will you be while I'm explaining this to Mr Kingcombe, Doctor?'

'I'll be hiding in the toilet, where he can't see me. When you're sure that he's gone, wait ten minutes then knock on the door. Four knocks.'

'You're sure.'

'Yes. I most certainly am.'

'Are you alright, Doctor? He's not *threatened you*, has he?'

'No, he hasn't. But I really don't want to explain why. Your sister, the one who works on reception at Scalby surgery…'

'Diane?'

'Doctor Waller at Scalby surgery had a case like this. A chap with the same issue as Mr Kingcombe. He was the landlord of the Shirestones Hotel. You will have to ask your sister Elaine whether she knows anything about Lindsay Boldwood from Doctor Waller. If they're willing to put you in the picture you'll know why I can't talk about it. Frankly, Elaine, I wish he'd never come here. That's all I'm going to say on the matter.'

'I'll go and tell him now. What if he wants to see someone else?'

'Say we've no more appointments today.'

'What shall I say if he wants to come back tomorrow?'

'Then tell him we've no more appointments for the week, for the month. Just get rid of him.'

'Doctor… should I call the police?'

'Not if you still want to be working here next month, no. And don't mention this to anyone. One other thing: find out where he's staying so we can send on his records. I don't want him back in this surgery as long as I'm living and breathing.'

'I'll do as you ask, Doctor.'

'I'm don't mean to be sharp to you, Elaine. But it's imperative you get him out of here as fast as possible.'

'He's not *dangerous* to *us*, is he, Doctor?'

'*No. Not until it gets dark…*'

Chapter Twelve

Set the Controls for the Heart of the Sun

Seeing that their hardest task was done, the Druid's menhir-hauling team took a tea break, whilst Pyrlig's exacting overseers checked the position of the stone relative to the central foundation pit. The hay cushions were removed from the pits and the first sack of hardcore chippings was pulled up to the lip of the ten-foot deep pit on its cart and emptied, bringing the depth up to eight feet after it was levelled. Two large bracing ropes leading off to the left and right were tied to chalk marks at quarter distance from the base, which now overhung the pit; a great leather strap, resembling a Shire horse collar studded with iron rings, was tied further up at the mid-point. More control ropes were added below the lift collar.

As the men split into their teams for the second stage of the lift, Pyrlig 'baptised' the stone and invited their bards to perform an ancient Welsh blessing. It was beautifully sung, absolutely indecipherable and deeply moving –so much so that some of the men had even stopped chewing their sausages; then Cadwallop got his chainsaw out, the teams put their gloves on and their audience stood up to clap and cheer.

The first log, supporting the broadest end of the megalith over the pit, was carefully cut under the eye of a spotter with an air horn, then both halves were quickly hauled out with by-ropes secured around their notched ends. Pyrlig raised his staff as a signal for the rope teams to brace as the chainsaw bit into the second log and the rope teams dug in their heels when the stone began to tip.

'Here she goes, Else, we ought to get one of these for the garden. Do you think we'd need planning permission?' asked Mark Cakebread.

'There's an idea. We could string Christmas lights around it!'

'We could.'

'We'd have every stray dog pissing on it.'

'We probably would.'

'Yeah, but we'd have real pagan cred.'

'I wonder if someone could mek us one in fibreglass... like them volcanoes at Dinosaur Land.'

'STEADY AS SHE GOES!' shouted Pyrlig. 'FRONT BASE PROP TEAM – BRACE AND HOLD!'

'Where's the loo, Vi?' pleaded Joy. 'I can't keep me legs crossed any longer...'

'Right side of the kitchen. It's a tent.'

'A tent!'

'Well, it's more of a teepee. The big blue one with the cardboard sign that sez "Ladies". Only one bum at a time, though.'

'TEN AND TWO O'CLOCK WAIST COLLAR TEAMS – HAUL UP!'

'I'm not going in a bucket!'

'It's a chair.'

'A chair?!'

'A chair with two of the seat slats missing – it's alright,

Joy, it's over a hole. With sawdust in it. When you've peed, just toss some more sawdust over the top, pet.'

'Are you serious?'

'It's better than the woods. We're next to the bloody woods, girl – in case you haven't noticed. It's not that bad.'

'You've tried it then, Vi?'

'Oh, aye. Just make sure you zip it up at the front.'

'The rocks upright, girls!' crowed Phyllis.

'FRONT BASE PROP TEAM, HOLD. FRONT WAIST TEAM, HOLD TENSION… PROP TEAMS TWO, THREE AND FOUR, GET READY TO BRACE FRONT AND SIDES AT TOP DEAD CENTRE. FRONT AND SIDE RUBBLE AND HARDCORE TEAMS, GET READY TO SPLIT YOUR BAGS! Bring me my plumb bob and stepladder.'

'What's top dead centre, Phyll?' asked Violet.

'It's like the middle of the, top I think. When it's straight… summat like that.'

'What are they doing with them big sacks?'

'Well, when it's up, they empty their sacks so it doesn't droop. Then they pound it – so it doesn't go floppy.'

'What are they pounding?'

'The hardcore stuff.'

Pyrlig ascended his old wooden stepladder with his plumb bob at all four cardinal points of the compass, carefully adjusting the stepladder prior to each check with his spirit level, adding packers and wedges from Jewson where necessary to ensure his angles were as accurate as required. Once he had checked the stone was true and upright he gave his next set of orders.

'RELEASE RUBBLE!'

'I haven't seen so many ropes and so many buff labourers since we went to see *Land of the Pharaohs* at the Odeon in Leicester Square, Phyll. Do you think Cadwallop looks like James Robertson Justice?'

'RELEASE HARDCORE!'

'I don't think James Robertson Justice was that handy with a chainsaw.'

'Pyrlig just looks like Catweazle.'

'*WELEASE BWIAN!*' yelled a comedian in the audience. Two of the hardcore and rubble team broke off to search for the blasphemer, who was quickly identified, bound, gagged and strapped to the roof of Cadwallop's Mitsubishi Shogun.

'BRING FORTH THE PLATE COMPACTOR! PEG YOUR BRACING LOGS TO MOTHER EARTH. ALL HANDS TO THE STONE!'

Cyn and Getafix dropped their ropes and strolled over to the witches to say hello and pass the time whilst the rest of their company laid hands on the megalith to prevent the vibrations of the plate compactor giving the stone the geological equivalent of a migraine.

'Aren't you needed over yonder, boys?' asked Joy, fresh from her trip to the teepee toilet.

'I've got a blister,' moaned Getafix.

'What about you, Cyn?'

'Got my fingers caught under a prop,' he muttered, holding out three sausage fingers with bruised black fingernails. 'Won't be holding any more mead tankards with this.'

'OOOH, that looks nasty, love. They're not broken, are they?' asked Violet, gritting her teeth.

'Don't think so. It just throbs a bit.'

'Get him a whisky, Joy… for his good hand. You better sit down, pet, while you're drinking it.'

'Thanks, Vi.'

'Can I have a whisky, girls?' asked Getafix.

'We're a bit low on whisky… pet,' said Joy. 'What about a rum, love, since it's only a blister? It'll have to be straight, we're low on Cola.'

'Umm…'

'Or you can have a vodka? We didn't pack a lot of soft drinks – we like the hard stuff.'

'Vodka, please. If that's okay.'

'Are you ill, Phyll?' asked Vi, noticing Phyllis had turned an unhealthy shade of Sherwood green.

'I think I'm going to be sick…'she mumbled, tottering off to the ladies'.

'Put some sawdust on it!' shouted Joy.

'You got a place to sit now too, lad – you and your vodka.' Violet grinned.

'It's a big bugger, ain't it, Vi?' commented Joy, looking Pyrlig's erection up and down. 'Even with a third of the fat end in the ground. When are they sinking the others around it?'

'There's four smaller ones coming tomorrow. The last of 'em, I think.'

'What about the other pits?'

'They're for fires. Then they fill 'em in.'

'So what's going in between?'

'Thin air, pet.'

'So it's not gonna be all joined up like a wagon wheel then. Like Stonehenge was?'

'Pyrlig says it's disrespectful to stick 'em all in Mother Earth at the same time.'

'I can smell venison, girls.'

'That'll get 'em excited. We could go over now and get ours before the rush – all this booze is giving me the munchies.'

'They're doing pie 'n' peas tonight.'

'OOOH, no. There's only one teepee on this plateau. Better not risk it.'

When the plate compactor was eventually switched off, the druids holding the menhir let out a huge sigh of relief and lowered their aching arms to get some blood back down to their fingers. Pyrlig and Belator thanked each man for their hard work and then ran their beady eyes over the stone to check that the compression of the rubble and hardcore had not induced any cracking, pronouncing the stone firm and intact. The team relaxed and stood back to admire the great stone in its new setting. Then Cacklog the chef banged his cymbal and a stampede of boots and beards rushed towards the caterers.

The acting chieftan of the East Yorkshire Ancient Warrior Society watched the druids charge on the caterers with a new respect. He was certainly grateful that they hadn't suggested a re-enactment of arms from the dark ages as a finale to the afternoon's labour. Some of their members had lost more than enough fingers already and there weren't enough ambulances in the whole of North Yorkshire for a real fight. Or even a pretend one.

Chapter Thirteen

A Night Like This

Dudley departed Aveyou Nympton and its small community surgery in a thunderous sulk, leaving Elaine the receptionist and the last three patients in no doubt of his opinions concerning the shortcomings of their hospitality.

The most polite summary of his parting speech was that it was curt, factual and straight to the point, if slightly less brutal from having most of the sharp edges removed by his Devonshire vowels.

Instead of wasting any more of his precious time talking to sex-obsessed doctors, Dudley drove to Whitborough to get a greater range of opinions on his bodily hair problems at some of the larger chemists and find out what over-the-counter preparations were available, before he made another appointment to see the family doctor back home in Devon.

He also resolved not to mention any of his other new urges for the rest of his stay, as the knowledge seemed to generate a palpable animus towards him from the few people he had told. A few hours spent in the town centre absent of gate posts, trees and telegraph poles, he reasoned, would also offer him some relief from the urge to cock his leg or sniff the air– as he felt compelled to do around the many canine marker points out in the suburbs –as well as giving him the chance to catch up on his shopping.

Feeling a little better after a walk through the town, Dudley stocked up at the local supermarket and then drove back to his rented chalet at Butlin's in Filey. He was starting to enjoy his new surroundings and had mixed feelings about returning to Devon. But now there was no longer a monster problem in North Yorkshire there was no more money either. In Devon there were still plenty of big cats to kill, a farm to run and a fiancée to disappoint. His parents would just have to accept that he wasn't going to commit to matrimonial suicide just to extend the family tree, because if Ella Furnish ever got on his branch, it would certainly have snapped.

That evening, he rang his parents in Honiton from the public bar at Butlin's to let them know that he would soon be coming home.

'Hello, Ma.'

'Oh, hello, Dud. Everything alroight up thurr, izzit?'

'Tiz now, Ma. Got the last o' their carnivores snug in a body bag. Nuthen' much to do yerr now so I thought I'd drop eee a line, let you an' Pa know oill be back soon. Oi jus' been taking a foo days rest afore oi set off back.'

'Oim'fraid oi got zome bad noos for eee son. Or it moight be good – in the fullness o'toime.'

'BAD NOOS?'

'Me an' Pa owe eee an apology, first of all. Trying to fix yoos up with that Ella Furnish. We had to ask'er to leave son. Turns out she's been seen trying ta smother the Calor Gas Man – and if that t'weren't reason enough, we 'eard she's bin planning to shack up with a bleddy fencing contractor frum Torrington. You wouldn't 'ave thought she'd have 'ad so many options. Looking loike she does…'

'She probably forced 'erself on 'em, Ma. Can't say I'm disappointed. Least it'll save me the trouble of having to shoot 'er when oi gets back.'

'Dudley!'

'Though oi moight 'ave needed a bigger gun than oi got. A few cannon shells moight have done the trick. Least the ewes an' the cattle won't be shivering with froight no more ev'ry toime they seen 'er coming. What you saw in 'er in the first place is a bleddy mystery to me, if you want the plain truth, but we'll say n'more about it. Oime just glad youze come round.'

'So when will eee be back, bay?'

'Couple o' days, Ma. I'll ring eee when I get ta the services near Taunton.'

'Truck's alroight, izzit?'

'Never misses a beat. I'll ring eee soon. Oi gotta go now, oi gotta take a shower.'

'Look after yourself, son. Be good to 'aveeee back.'

Dudley decided it would be a waste of time packing away his shopping in the chalet's kitchen cupboards on the last night of his stay, so he left his shopping bags on the long worktop beside the sink. He'd only eaten scraps since blasting Albert Gall's head from his shoulders in Cloughton's historic Norman churchyard and he had to admit that he just didn't have the desire to cook or eat a proper meal. If the male menopatch wasn't responsible for his loss of appetite then he really didn't know what to do next – or who to ask. The chemists in Whitborough had not been as helpful as he had hoped they might be. They didn't want to spare the time to look at his hands and feet – or his ears. They had shown very little inclination to help him at all; perhaps his accent was too deep and too strange. Perhaps his old army clothing had convinced them he was a penniless hobo. He had given up and decided to go back to Butlin's, read his mail and the *Honiton Gazette* then take a shower before retiring to bed.

Perhaps his appetite would return the next morning.

Just before his shower, Dudley phoned Constable Alger at home in Kettleness to ask him if he'd like to inspect the headless werewolf body parts in the freezer inside his truck before he left the next day. He had already been paid for his first night's hunting, unsuccessful though it was, as compensation for being run down by Alger's Land Rover. The contract he'd signed with Kettleness Parish Council had not specified how many predators there were in their locality, but it did demand he eradicate their predator 'problem'. Even though his host had killed Lindsay Boldwood before he got to him himself,

Dudley felt perfectly justified in invoicing them for two, once he had tracked and executed Albert. He had never had a problem getting paid for hunting big cats or werewolves; nobody he had ever spoken to in the many accounts departments he communicated with had ever wanted to critique the invoices of someone who works out of a gun cabinet.

Chapter Fourteen

Hi-de-Hi-de-Hi
Ho-de-Ho-de-Howl
Go, Go, Go, Do the Holiday Rock

Mercifully for Dudley, his first transformation from bandy-legged farmer to bandy-legged monster of legend took place in the privacy of the shower cubicle in his rented holiday chalet at Butlin's – and not in the driver's cab of his Bedford truck or a public house toilet.

The entire ordeal went about as well as these things do when they occur. He was already undressed and preparing for a shower – always a blessing in the circumstances– and nowhere near a gas fire, or an electric toothbrush.

The shower head was safely out of reach above his bald patch, the tiles of the shower cubicle were thick and stout and mortared directly onto ribbed concrete blocks, and the shower bottom was the kind of heavy-duty bomb-proof sanitary ware that the British used to do so well. It would certainly not show any signs of his panicky attempts to flee the shower and its soapy puddle once his claws had reached their full size.

The only thing that didn't stand up too well to his angry thrashing was the shower curtain, which looked as if it had been sucked into the blades of a combine harvester.

Once he had escaped the torrents of hot water and shaken himself dry Dudley cantered into the lounge and tried to make sense of his strange surroundings in his strange new body. He had gone up to nearly 450 pounds under the water and was now around six feet from his jowls to his hocks. He had also gained a huge hairy quiff between his ears which gave him a slightly comic appearance. On the minus side there was nothing at all amusing about his new fangs and hideous yellow eyes.

The safe end was still as comically broad and bandy-legged as its human equivalent, but it had gained a tail in the process that resembled an enormous fox's brush.

Dudley's neighbours, the owners of a holiday kennels business in the West Midlands, had turned off 'Annie's Song' by John Denver because Dudley's howls and pitiful whines had filled up their senses and were enough to put them off a night in the forest for a very long time indeed. It was very clear to them that all was not well with the dog next door, if it was indeed a dog – and their last doubts about their neighbour's cruelty disappeared when Dudley put his paw on the sharp edge of a Lego brick.

'Roight. That's it, we're calling the RSPCA, Sonya. God knows what that lot o' bastards are doing wi' that poor animal in there.'

'They're shut now, aren't they, Bill? The RSPCA? I don't think they work nights, luv.'

'Oh, bugger it…We'll call the police.'

'Hang on, luv. That RSPCA chap that lives over the road just came back. Go and ask 'im if he'll investigate.'

'Excuse me, but moi woife an' oi are really worried about the dog next door. We've bin hearing some really terrible noises and howls from their lounge. It's really, really distressin', we're at our wits' end.'

'Are you in one of these chalets beside the road, sir?'

'Number 2b, just across from you, Inspector. I'm on holiday, with me woife. We've got our own boarding kennels business. In Dudlay.'

'I can certainly ask. The noises are only coming from the chalet attached to you, are they, in 2a?'

'Yis, yis, they are. We'd be ever so grateful, Inspector, as a fellow animal lover. We can't take much more o' this tonight.'

'Okay. Well, I've just come off shift but I'll try them now while I'm still in uniform. I can't guarantee they'll let me in but at least you can call the police if it persists later on.'

'We'd be very grateful, we would. Thanks ever so much, Inspector.'

'Are their curtains drawn?'

'Not when we got in. He just had a table lamp on. There's just the net curtains.'

'He?'

'We've only seen one chap in there. That's his army lorry.'

'Is he the one—'

'With the bandy legs. That's him.'

'Have you seen his dog?'

'No. Not yet. But whatever kind of breed it is he's got in there, it must be a big 'un.'

Tony Barnes, Filey's only RSPCA inspector, wasn't overwhelmed with problem pet owners. Especially in the winter months when the holiday camps emptied. He was more often in Whitborough on Sea than on his own patch and so when the odd new case presented itself just outside his normal working hours he didn't ignore it out of habit until the following day.

When he arrived at the front of chalet 2a he found it was clean, tidy, free of litter and absent of the usual clues that the occupant owned a pet. There was no dog bowl on the planks of the small balcony and no small towels, toys or harness hanging from any of the coat hooks.

The occupants had left the curtains open but the nets were drawn. There was some brightness from the bathroom doorway beyond the back wall of the lounge coming through the connecting hall, but the lounge was otherwise gloomy. Only the feeble light of a small table lamp on a bookshelf revealed the dim outlines of the furniture within. Inspector Barnes knocked on the door and then stood back to listen. There wasn't any audible response within so he repeated his well-practised raps for the second time, but still no one came to answer the door and the lights inside remained dim.

Before he tried knocking on the door one last time, he stood down from the balcony and walked across the large front window which stretched the full width of the lounge, just to see if he could identify any figure or movement, however indistinct. Everything looked calm and still. As the inspector's eyes adjusted in the shadows he began to realise there was something rather large and intimidating in front of what he guessed was a sofa. It was about the height of a rocking horse, with a worryingly familiar outline. The last time he had seen its double, it had been stalking a zebra in the African bush on BBC2.

Before he could get into his pocket for his camera, whatever it was had leapt through the middle pane of the large glass window, bashed his head on its descent to terra firma and disappeared into the shadows behind the lower row of bungalows, leaving a distinct aroma of wet dog and Shake 'n' Vac.

Dudley's next-door neighbours, who were bunched up behind their curtains, saw everything from the far side of their own lounge window, but they still couldn't quite believe the evidence from their own eyes.

It seemed they had left the safety of their home and the dogs for a mini-break with a werewolf, and it was certainly a heck of a lot bigger and meaner than anything either Hollywood or Hammer Films had ever imagined. God knows where it had come from – or where it had gone – but it had, for the moment, disappeared. Shaking with terror, Mr Lofthouse and his wife eventually regained enough self-control and enough small pips of courage to drag the poor unconscious RSPCA inspector off the grass and back into the relative safety of their bungalow, bolting the door before the monster next door came back to finish him off.

'We can't ring the police for that thing! They'll think we're mad! What are we going to do, Bill…?We can't stay here with that thing out there.'

'Too roight we're not staying here. Pack the bags, luv. We're leaving.'

'What are we going to do about this poor man? We can't just leave him here.'

'See which pocket his van keys are in. I'll carry him back to his van, he'll be alroight in there.'

'He's got a cut on his head, Bill.'

'Just give it a woipe.'

'I'll put some Dettol on it.'

'Make it quick, Sonya. While I'm putting him in the van, pack all the cases. Fast as you can. We'll send the key back in the mail once we're 'ome.'

'Are we taking the food in the fridge?'

'Just them pork pies. They're luvley, them. Or they moight be if moi bloody appetite ever comes back.'

'I'll take 'em for the dogs.'

Bill and Sonya's dogs were far enough away from Dudley Kingcombe to be sure of getting a good night's sleep, but the dogs in the chalets and caravans on the park were far from happy. Any pet owner who had left a window ajar had unwittingly allowed the scent of every poor canine's worst nightmare to drift into the safety of their holiday homes. Within the space of a few minutes televisions and radios were drowned out by the howls of terrified dogs warning other dogs, as cats cried to be let indoors and all the hedgehogs in the park scampered back under the caravans to squeeze themselves into the tightest spaces they could find.

Some of the owners made the mistake of opening their doors to listen to the canine chorus, sending their dogs over the edge, until they realised the panic they were causing their beloved friends and swiftly locked their doors again.

Just one man, on his way back to his caravan from the off-licence, saw Dudley in all his glory, but he put it down to drink. His beery breath and the smell of spilt drink undoubtedly saved him from being eaten alive. The next man waiting at the camp's bus stop was not quite so lucky. By the time his bus arrived at the bus stop outside the park gates there wasn't enough of him left to put in a pedal bin liner. The driver immediately drove off to the police station and rushed inside with two other passengers to inform the duty officer there had been another grisly murder and give them the location of the remains of the deceased.

As the canine chorus at Butlin's settled down to a few whimpers, Dudley ran north from the camp, crossing the railway line, and then ran along the banking before taking to the fields towards the bright lights of Filey, entering the town close to the beach. A few minutes later, he made another corpse around the back of the offices of the Filey branch of Bee Hive Taxis, eating a member of the waiting staff at the Esplanade Hotel, who had nipped behind their dustbins to relieve himself. He also killed a fibreglass polar bear on the green, took a bite out of a Colonel Sanders effigy beside Kentucky Fried Chicken and chased some sea cadets into the bus station toilets. The boys managed to bolt themselves inside one of the cubicles but Dudley at least had the compensation of eating the vandal who was smashing up the Tic-Tac mints dispenser. He was a skinny wretch, dressed in a vile shell suit that was as indigestible in the gut as it was on the eyes, but he would bother the good citizens of Filey no more. None except the toilet cleaner, who was astonished that anybody could have had such a gigantic nosebleed on his tiles and yet not use any of the toilet roll in the cubicles to stop it.

Feeling satisfied with his foray into Filey, Dudley retraced his route to Butlin's and bedded down for the night in the old donkey stables a hundred yards away from his truck. When he woke before dawn it was as a human. Very confused, but no longer in need of a good square meal, he managed to sneak into the back of his lorry without being seen, then grabbed a camouflage poncho and ran back into the chalet to get another shower.

He dressed, packed his bags and went to reception to settle up.

'Mornen. Oive come to settle up, maid. Thurrs me key.'

'Good morning, Mr Kingcombe, is it?'

'Thass me. 2a. Near the main road.'

'Has everything been alright for you, sir?'

'Up until this mornen'. I stayed out last night, when I got back yerr I found me front window smashed and the shower curtains missen'.'

'Oh, I am sorry. Have you lost anything? Shall I call the police?'

'No, oi 'aven't lost a thing. Place is spic 'n' span. Except for the shower curtain, course. No need to call the police on my account. Just petty vandalism, oi reckon t'was.'

'Well, if you're sure—'

'How much is it, maid, me meter's still a foiver in credit, mind.'

'We can't give refunds on meter credit, Mr Kingcombe. I'm sorry.'

'Never moind. Least ways youze got a noo shower curtain out of me.'

'The total owing is two hundred and ten pounds, Mr Kingcombe, for fourteen nights. We have to retain your deposit for the cost of the glass, sir. There's no other damage, Mr Kingcombe?'

'Just the big window. You might wanna get it fixed sharpish. Afore it rains.'

Inspector Tony Barnes woke up in his RSPCA van a full half hour after Dudley Kingcombe had driven away. He had fallen sideways onto the passenger seat soon after being placed in his van the night before and as a result he'd developed a little bit of stiffness and cramp. He started to ease himself upright and pushed the seat back on its rails to stretch his legs whilst he tried to piece together the events of the previous evening through the pain of a throbbing headache. He snapped down the sun visor and was horrified to see a deep red scratch from his hairline to his eyebrow and a smaller scratch on his cheek. He remembered talking to a couple about a dog howling but couldn't quite recall much else. Had he been mugged? He still had his wallet. A quick check revealed nothing had been taken and the keys for the van had been put in the cup holder recess behind the gear lever. It was all a bit strange. He opened the van door and stepped out slowly, testing his other limbs for any sign of further injury, but he appeared to be fully fit apart from his new scars. He could find nothing else to indicate what had happened to him the night before, until he discovered the smear of mud and grass on the back of his jacket and trousers. He had a shower, a change of clothes and made himself a big mug of coffee then sat down in his recliner and let his mind drift. No other memories came – and slowly, he fell asleep.

Chapter Fifteen

Synchronicity

Quetzlcarbon Yum Taxx, Mayan fire demon extraordinaire, was now just two gold doubloons away from some well-earned rest and peace and quiet in Hell. He'd had 438 blissful years of it since the treasure he had been tasked with guarding had been buried on a plateau overlooking Cayton Bay.

One might reasonably ask what business a Mayan demon has, guarding Spanish gold in a cold corner of North Yorkshire, but history has a thousand examples of one culture stealing from another and getting into all sorts of bother – and that's without swapping one's native diseases and viruses in wars of conquest. Or the modern method, international student exchanges.

The Mayans, like the ancient dynasties of Egypt, had accumulated so much gold they were compelled to create a whole new class of professional sorcerers and seers to write curses to protect it, and there were so many curses that they were compelled to embark on an endless temple-building programme to increase the space to record them. When the foot soldiers of the Empire of Spain took home plundered Mayan gold, they also imported many Mayan curses and their attendant Mayan demons, who were tumbling off their galleons by the hundred in Cadiz, Lisbon, Bilbao and Valencia.

Until the holders of the last scraps of the treasure of the Mar del Norte returned their cursed coins to the plateau above Cayton Bay by accident or conscious intention, Yum Taxx was compelled to maintain his campaign of vandalism and arson before he could get back into Hell. Until then, he had no option but to suffer an eternity of misery in Yorkshire, trying to start fires in desks and damp sheds full of chicken manure. But a very strange conjunction of events was soon to deliver a most fortuitous and unexpected deliverance.

The coin with which Yum Taxx had blackened the bureau of Lord William Henry Warner Woollens was now in his lordly pocket and heading for the second day of henge construction at Cayton Bay. Lord William Henry, an avid student of local history with the best library in the county, knew exactly what he had got and what he was compelled to do with it. As a man who was already very bushy about the chin and temples, he was at no risk of looking out of place.

The other doubloon was also on its way home. It had seen quite a lot of the world since leaving Maureen's house inside Bert, her Parsons terrier. Maureen had hoped it might have been recovered at the vet, courtesy of the vet's finger, but the vet's finger had followed the coin after Bert had severed it and fled Bellend Vet's examination room. Fate had brought dog and coin to the BADCOW punk-rock commune in Burniston and into the possession of Stigg, Bert's new bestie and poo picker-upper. Without going into too much detail about how it was restored to its previously shiny condition, it was now in a slightly less pongy place at the bottom of Stigg's Doc Marten boot – and quite safe from being disturbed, being in the last place anyone who was not called Stigg would want to go.

With no immediate need to burn down the BADCOW Scout hut or attack Charlwood's outbuildings, Yum Taxx returned to the plateau at Cayton Bay and waited on events inside the mouth of an abandoned Badger set. He could do nothing to influence events until darkness fell, but there was now the real possibility his work would soon be done. He might even manifest his Mayan sky warrior alter ego again. It had certainly impressed one young druid already.

Chapter Sixteen

Gangsters

Ted Knight's unopposed restoration to the position of Whitborough on Sea's foremost psychopath had little immediate impact in a town cursed by terrorism, arson, exploding nightclubs and murderous supernatural predators when added to all its other misfortunes.

His status was only an issue for his brother-in-law – Whitborough's chief of police, Superintendent Ascoyne D'Ascoyne –whose team of detectives had been unable to find any witness or evidence to identify the criminals responsible for the theft and burning of his beloved black Mercedes 280 saloon.

It was almost inevitable that the two MI5 agents sent to monitor the police investigation into the terrorist attack were listening in on Superintendent D'Ascoyne's private line when his gangster brother-in-law called to inform him the official investigation into the theft of his car was now over and a contract had been issued by Club-Land's mafia for the capture and torture of the culprits.

Two large glasses of Baileys had failed to smother the spread of D'Ascoyne's paranoia and insecurity that now rose to a level which matched the resentment and jealously and the increasing sense of panic he had endured since his two best detectives had signed off sick. His hopes of a smooth upward climb to early retirement were looking more and more like a distant dream. He could do himself no harm by getting some urgent advice from a friend who had experienced many troubles of his own. It was time to call on his friend the chief constable, so he locked up his drawers, remembering to place some hair from his wife's hairbrush onto the top of each drawer face, blew some fine talcum powder on the underside of the filing cabinet grips and left his office with his journal.

On the way out of the building he suddenly had one of his rare moments of inspiration. The idea that came to him would certainly put his unwelcome guests from MI5 and the Home Office in the same quicksand that he had been forced to wade in since all the trouble began and force them to put some skin in the game. It might even save him from becoming their fall guy. Marshall and Broadhead had already outplayed the Home Office team, plotting against them by pulling a sickie, even though unofficially they were still 'working the case'. D'Ascoyne couldn't use the same trick. He was going to have to use all his reserves of cunning. He decided to give MI5 and their friends from the Home Office the ghost tape he had seen Broadhead watching and then send them to Charlwood House for a history lesson from Lord William Henry Warner Woollens that would take the wind out of their sails.

The records and evidence room at Whitborough Police Station was deep in the basement of the building. It had all the charm of a morgue. There were no windows or soft chairs or pictures to relieve the impersonal atmosphere of solitary confinement. Bleached by harsh, fluorescent strip lights, the grotto of steel and plastic was even less welcoming than the cells. It was nicknamed 'Barry's Bunker' after the sergeant, who had cheerfully managed it for five long years. Superintendent D'Ascoyne had only ever visited it twice. On both occasions, he had been only too glad to leave. But when he descended the steps for his third visit it was as a man who had just had a great burden lifted from his shoulders. He actually had a spring in his step.

'Ah! Sergeant!'

'Good morning, sir,' replied the sergeant with a slight accent of surprise.

'Do you have the tape of the, er, *disturbance* in reception? I believe Marshall and Broadhead signed it out recently.'

'They took both copies, sir. But they haven't brought them back.'

'Both copies… are there only two?'

'The ghost tape?'

'Yes, Sergeant, the "ghost tape". Do you have a third copy?'

'In the safe, sir.'

'Excellent. Make me two copies.'

'Now, sir?'

'Yes. While it's copying, get me the Manor Farm files on the Hoopers for 1940–65.'

'Inspector Marshall signed them out, sir.'

'I'll need a key for his office then and his cabinets.'

'Have you watched the tape, sir?'

'Broadhead played me some of it.'

'What did you make of it, sir?'

'I'd say it's just the kind of evidence we need to show our new "guests" from the Home Office, Sergeant, and I'm going to make sure they get to see it.'

'What are your thoughts on the matter? You've watched it yourself, I presume?'

'I didn't much like it, in all honesty. But I can't fault your thinking, sir. Stick it to 'em, if you'll pardon my expression.'

'Thank you very much, Sergeant.'

'I'll be glad when this business is over and done with, sir, then we get our station back. I don't think your new guests like sharing our burden either, to tell you the truth. But I don't think they're the kind of people I'd like to have as friends…'

'I know just what you mean.'

Once he had set his trap. He drove home feeling rather pleased with himself. He couldn't do much about his mad gangster brother-in-law's habitual impulse for violence, but he wasn't going to keep it a secret. Wisely, he had always taped their phone calls and made duplicates. The conversation implicating Ted Knight as the instigator of the contract on the Mercedes thieves was also delivered to the Home Office. He made two more, sending one to Inspector Marshall, and stored the other copy at home.

Chapter Seventeen

The Spy Who Taped Me

MI5's MACE1 agent Captain James Stocke was not at all happy with the way his investigation had been progressing since arriving in Whitborough on Sea from London. His subordinate Bruce Keogh was similarly frustrated. Their lodgings at Bronte's Rest, overlooking the sea cadet's parade ground, were pleasant enough, but neither man had been able to develop any new leads or add any new information to what was already a fairly comprehensive case file to justify their new status as MACE field operatives.

London's decision to send a team to install covert listening devices in the offices and homes of Detective Inspector Marshall and Superintendent D'Ascoyne had already backfired.

Inspector Marshall had surprised them all with his natural intelligence and cunning, guessing their moves and deftly blunting their eavesdropping with a mixture of local radio and a who's who of country and western. Inspector Marshall was also, they were discovering, very shrewd. He was a man who could see the big picture in an incomplete summary of evidence and identify his place in it with an uncanny precision. He was also not the kind of policeman who was going to share his suspicions with anyone above him if he suspected they were going to diminish or ignore his contribution at a successful conclusion when the plaudits were handed out.

He had also anticipated his new status in the hierarchy of scapegoats, in front of Superintendent D'Ascoyne, and then outplayed his enemies by signing off sick.

Thanks to the stupidity of their bosses in London, Stocke and Keogh had lost their best in-house link to likely leads and with it all the local knowledge that they so desperately needed to move forward.

There had been precious little warmth towards them from the moment they had arrived at Whitborough on Sea's police station with the other teams from the MOD and the Home Office, with their secrecy, their inflated sense of entitlement, titles and private agendas. It was the kind of thoughtless, clumsy imposition that was guaranteed to create bad blood between guest and host. Instead of a unified, formidable investigation unit of complementary services, there were now two camps plotting against themselves. The police on one side, and MI5, the MOD and the Home Office on the other, but the biggest block to the progress of the investigation had been the public themselves. No one, it seemed, had been willing to enlighten either the police or their uninvited guests.

Hollow Hills Farm, the semi-derelict former home of the Hooper Farming Mafia, had been searched twice and revealed nothing.

The two traffic patrolmen who had investigated the strange gathering on the plateau above Cayton Bay had clammed up and refused to add anything to their statements.

The interview with the Horsforth Sixth Form History teacher Mr Shannon, who had fired the siege cannon at HMS *Heddon*, had failed to uncover evidence that he was associated with any prescribed terrorist organisations. It had also been painfully slow (as his hearing and continence had still not returned) and those questions that weren't assisted with photographs or crude sign language had to be worked out through Post-It notes at Wold Newton prison, where he was being held on remand.

Unfortunately for Mr Shannon, the Defence Secretary had ordered an investigation into his affairs and the Home Office were able to present evidence revealing he had taken a holiday with his girlfriend in East Germany; he also had a subscription to *Socialist Worker*, which was more than enough for judge and jury to set a tariff of thirty years with no parole.

The staff at BOL D'OR Motorcycles could not identify the terrorist who had machine-gunned two patrol cars and a police BMW motorcycle at Carr Wold Parkway before he stole a customer's Kawasaki GPZ1100 from their workshop.

No one at the Four Horseman Mexican Cantina had seen a thing. Agents Stocke and Keogh were, however, convinced that a revenge attack against Hector the chef was just a matter of time.

Inside Whitborough Police Station, there was an atmosphere of hopelessness and dread. With no leads and no evidence, the investigation had ground to a halt. The wedge of holiday request forms submitted after Inspector Marshall's outburst and suspension – at the very first joint briefing – had been the beginning of the end.

Careers and reputations now hung by a thread. They waited for sentencing, on the whim of the Home Secretary and the Secretary of State for Defence.

The press had put its heel on the neck of the Government and the pressure had become intolerable. The Navy had lost a Destroyer and a Lynx Helicopter, Whitborough had lost its mayor and mayoress, and the police had taken a severe battering – even with the help of the Territorial Army, yet only one arrest had been made. The Government (as the ultimate authority responsible for the Royal Navy) was also in the sights of a class-action lawsuit brought by the survivors of the Milk Race Massacre, against elements of the crew of HMS *Heddon*.

1MACE (Mass Casualty Events), status special agent. Pay & benefits Band 5.

Chapter Eighteen

The Landkey Sorceress Rides Out

Four miles off the coast on Landkey Island, in Weareburgh Grange, Sveta Anchabadze and her servants were packing for a twenty-four-hour working trip to the mainland.

The alarming visions and messages from her spirit guides necessitated an urgent visit to Cayton Bay, where a build-up of antagonistic psychic forces was threatening to erupt into a clash between old gods, old forces, uppity demons and the followers of their opposing tribes.

The plateau had long been associated with the followers of the old religion for several millennia and then very slowly, the cauldron rituals of the druids had given way to the chalice rituals of the practitioners of Wicca. The Wiccans were still active but rather annoyed by the sudden arrival of the Black Hand Coven, who made up for their technical shortcomings and lack of experience with two spectacularly catastrophic rituals, the last of which had killed all the grass and weeds in a circle a hundred and twenty feet across.

Quite by chance, a band of local druid revivalists had decided the new bald patch was a sign that their gods thought the plateau would look even better with a big rock calendar on it. Their forefathers had pretty much covered the best sites on Landkey and the UK mainland even before the Romans arrived, but, just like Barratt, Beavers and Taylor Wimpey, proper druids live to build.

The druids were clearly going to win. They had *old* gods, they had new boots and, more importantly, they had a field kitchen. They were big, hairy and scary, but they also had the freedom to conduct their activities without any need for concealment. They could pick their noses, defecate in trenches, burp, fart and drink past the point of collapse, lie naked on a menhir and no one ever raised a single objection. The more earthy they were, it seemed, the more the public adored them. This enraged the Satanists, who couldn't even write their religion on a life insurance application form.

Sveta Anchabadze's only concern was reducing the amount of casualties and protecting her former paramour. Despite his record, she still had some residual affection for him and saw that he was in the process of repentance. And not only because it was costing him an arm and a leg in expensive gifts to keep his second wife on side.

Sveta didn't 'do' modern forms of transport but she had three loyal horses, Tolstoy, Alexei and Pushkin, from the wild herd on Landkey that she often called upon to carry her and her shopping. She and her two servants were forced to wait for low tide before they could walk the horses across the causeway that linked the island to the mainland. They bought lunch and several gin and tonics in the Briny Ewe public house in the harbour, collecting seaweed, three lobsters and two large crabs from the rock pools beside the causeway for their afternoon meal to eat with the homemade bread that Sveta cooked in her old iron range.

Once on the mainland they shopped for other essentials unavailable on the island, stocking up on sewing needles, light bulbs, matches and stamps, setting off for Cayton Bay three miles south as the shops were closing.

On the plateau, the druids were admiring the result of their final day of hard labour. The installation of four tall rock 'fingers' aligned to the four points of the compass around their central mehir. The remaining pits were heaped with logs over the ash from the barbecue and set alight.

Pyrlig, the chief druid, performed a short ceremony of blessing and directed younger legs to tie a high white ribbon around the central menhir, then more lengths were run from the centre to the four finger stones in the outer circle and woven garlands of willow and zinnia flowers placed upon their tops. Finally, Belator poured a cup of mead over the base of each stone to help it settle in the earth.

Chapter Nineteen

My People Were Fair and Had Sky in Their Hair…
But Now They're Content to Wear Stars
on Their Brows

Sir William Henry Warner Woollens had never accepted anything for his wardrobe in the category of smart casual. He was a traditionalist to his toes. Lamb's wool pullovers, chinos and yachting shoes were definitely not his cup of tea. Three-piece tweed suits, tailored shirts and Gladstone boots were the only things he ever wore, except when testing the family's collection of historic experimental weapons on the rear lawns of Charlwood House. On these occasions, he was always seen in full armour with a closed helm.

The family had a long, proud history of creating the machinery of sudden violent death. Their WWGB brand had helped outnumbered Britons in tight spots across the world blast their enemies into the afterlife, leaving battlefields around the globe as quiet and lifeless as a Roman catacomb.

A Warner Woollens had built the very first trebuchet and died at its first test. His ancestor had created an eight-barrelled rotating siege gun and was buried with a full honour guard in eight caskets of descending size next to the graves of the war commission's witnesses. It may well have inspired Richard Jordan Gatling to create the Gatling gun in 1862 during the

American Civil War. Another Warner Woollens, Benjamin Stanley produced the prototype of a multi-barrelled mortar than preceded the German Nebelwerfer and the infamous Russian 'Stalin Organ', solving the nuisance of an issue of succession by shelling a folly used by his brother.

Sir William's own contribution to population control (apart from Charlwood Zoo's lions, tigers and wolves) was his gas-powered lightweight repeating crossbow. He had hoped for a grant from the Ministry of Defence to develop it for use by British Special forces, but an accident had necessitated a hospital admission for a member of the MOD's research and development team, whose screams had caused a crash in the cafe car park.

With such a history of arms, it was odd indeed that the most dangerous thing Lord William Henry had ever possessed was a small coin, made of gold, and he had now arrived in the place of its discovery. Before he could be interrupted, the Lord of Charlwood walked to the edge of the druid's circle, took out his Bowie knife from his shoulder holster and plunged it into the turf. He then checked he was still alone, gave the knife a little wiggle, dropped the coin in the gash and then stamped the turf back into place once he had drawn out his knife. He replaced his knife, rubbed his hands and set sail for the druids' field kitchen.

'Lord William, how very good to see you, sir,' said Cacklog warmly. 'We've still got some venison or wild boar steaks left, m'Lord. Or sausages made with thyme and oats?'

'Good heavenses, it smells delicious, Cacklog! May I have a sausage?'

'It's two per bap, sir. Onions and roasted peppers?'

'All the trimmings… It smells wondiferish!'

'How's the zoo, sir?'

'Quite secure now, Cacklog. We had a few wolves breakout, you probably heard about it in the *Whitborough Evening News*, no doubt. An intwooder opened their p-pen. We lost twoo of our ph-pheasants. But no children were eaten. Our insurers weren't pleased… but who gives a damn about them, eh? Paperwork, paperwork, paperwork… Do you know, I so warely get a good sa-sauasage at home,' he added. 'Is my old friend Pyrlig with us tonight?'

'He is, my Lord.'

'Excellent. Where does he sit when he's on duty?'

Smelly Bert, Whitborough on Sea's filthiest Parsons terrier, was now best pals with Stinky Stigg, the punk-rock landowner of the Burniston-based Anarchist collective BADCOW. They had become inseparable since they had found each other behind an empty Heineken keg at the back of Burniston's Three Jolly Morris Men public house.

To Stigg's great delight, Bert had seen off their self-appointed 'General Secretary' Mary Shipley Brown, their humourless, hard-left commander-in-chief, by dragging his bum across her pillows and scattering her tampons. He'd also left something resembling a caramel Mr Whippy in the house of Gemini, on her signs of the Zodiac quilt cover.

His determination to assert his territorial dominance had been one last insult too many for 'Anarchy Mary', who'd already had quite enough bad luck since moving from her family villa into the scout hut of her proletariat dreams.

Bert had also proved to be a fine guard dog, alerting Stigg to the presence of Albert Gall's werewolf in time to save their goats and chickens. Bert was never going to give up meat and become a vegetarian, but as he had always been a dog, it wasn't the issue it might have been.

Stigg and Bert had decided to visit Cayton Bay, to enjoy the druids' topping-out ceremony and marvel at the first new stone circle in Whitborough since the dark ages with Penny and Gary from BADCOW. As firm fans of alternative culture, they were quite keen to see some real druids and compare them with the memories of the sketches and drawings they'd grown up with in school. It was also a chance to try some mead and compare its strength to the lethal dishwater scrumpy they'd had at Glastonbury.

Chapter Twenty

Luck Be a Lady Tonight

With such a prestigious gathering of souls – and just one coin from safety – the last night of the druids was certainly going to be a memorable occasion for those carefully restricting their intake of mead. Heads were sore and muscles ached, but the druids' achievement was plain for all to see. When it came to rock sculpture, they were damn good at getting it up.

Their monuments could never hope to compete with the scale and sophistication of the ancient empires straddling the Earth's equator, but the men of Egypt and Rome never had to put up with freezing horizontal rain and thieving Saxons. No Mayan or Aztec had ever come home to burnt roundhouse with no wife and no tea. And no Egyptian stonemason had ever come home to find a Viking axe in the head of his best cow.

The druids of Britain could proudly say (in consonant-heavy words, inflected with a paste of grit) that they had left their mark on the British Isles as firm and lasting as the Pyramids on the Giza plateau –even though Stonehenge was a just a little bit wonky.

No one who was now in Valhalla had ever worried that their tomb wasn't level. They were too busy enjoying the afterlife.

Stigg and friends were delighted to discover that Cacklog, Cai and Mary still had veggie burgers – and buns to go with them. Bert got so excited when Stigg gave him a wild boar steak that he ran off into the woods so nobody could take it away from him, but there was something about the badger set nearby that was giving him goosebumps. He retraced his steps with even more speed than his first sprint and found a safe place under the tea urn table to finish up his tea.

The only other furry creature on the plateau with a collar was Brinsley the cat. He was a cat that knew his own mind and was seldom at home, as he was still in the first flush of youth, unlike his mama Violet, who had flushed most of hers away with wine and spirits and men and magic. Violet was a little too independently minded for Brinsley's simple tastes and he had always been careful to keep a little distance. For many weeks, he had not wanted to go home and risk being whisked away to another one of her woodland gatherings – for a second bath in demonic bodily fluids. His fur had only just started to grow back from the first time.

He had found comfortable alternative accommodation in an old badger set in Kenwith Woods, where food delivered itself and his sleeps were blissfully peaceful. There were no slamming doors, hair dryers and long telephone conversations punctuated by his mama's cackling and sudden shrieks of laughter. Nor were there any strange men in his house. In Kenwith Woods, there was only him and his prey. That was until another demon squeezed itself into his domain. And there was something else too. It was the smell of a dog.

As the sun sank lower towards a bright orange sunset and the final orders for barbecued meats petered out, the backlit forms of three riders on horseback could be seen approaching from the west, languidly threading their way down the ridge between the two bays. The leading rider appeared to be mounted side saddle.

The horses were as calm and composed as their mounts and almost seem to float as they descended to the gentler contours of the track, clearly heading towards the stone circle.

Bert seemed to sense something interesting in the manner of the lead rider and kept popping out from underneath Cacklog's table like a tortoise that had heard a rustling newspaper. His little darts became more and more frequent until he was practically dancing for joy. To the surprise of his human companions he suddenly darted towards Stigg, leant heavily on his ankle and cocked his leg, firing a warm stream of wee into the loose front gusset of Stigg's Doc Marten boot.

'AWWW, BERT! WHADDYA DOIN'!'

His friends began to giggle, grinning ever wider as their mate shook his foot and tried to pull off the wet boot before his sock turned dark.

'What's the matter with you! I just bought you a wild boar steak, you little git!' groaned Stigg, tossing aside the wet Doc Marten. Before anybody could react, Bert snatched up the boot and ran off toward the figure on the nearest horse, wagging his tail furiously.

'Where's he going now?' complained Stigg, finding himself one DM short of a walk home.

'Well, whoever they are, they must have pretty tasty dog biscuits, Stigg,' replied Penny. 'Do you want to borrow one of my spare pumps until Ms Pale Rider brings your boot back?'

'Yeah please, Penn. Thanks. How do you know they're a she, like?'

'Girls know these things, Stigg.'

'They're riding side saddle, Stigg,' added Gary.

'It's a girl thing. 'Penny grinned.

'So, she's come Belator,' observed Pyrlig, taking a long draw on his pipe as he watched Sveta Anchabadze and her two servants approach.

'To bless the stone?'

'The Sorceress of Landkey doesn't come off her island for trifles like that, old friend. I suspect she believes there's going to be some kind of reckoning later. I have my suspicions it might be connected to those low Coven people. They never were very good at leaving a clean table. But they're won't be any more of their nonsense here from now on. I imagine the Lady of Landkey has come to do a final wipe-down for us. Get rid of a few cobwebs – if you follow me? The old gods can't be expected to sit on a lumpy sofa.'

'THERE WERE DEMONS HERE!'

'What, my old friend, kills grass – as sure as darkness? It's one reason we've built here. One reason. *To drive them out.* And here is our cleaning lady, to finish the floors and kick out the last squatter. Observe our mistress…'

The woman in black dismounted her horse and crouched down to a very friendly Parsons terrier bearing gifts. Bert dropped Stigg's Doc Marten, which was taken up by Sveta and turned upside down and shaken. Bert backed away slightly, still wagging furiously, and then sat down, never once taking his gaze away from the strange lady in the long black dress and shawl.

Sveta took out a small silver blade and plunged it into

the turf, took the small object from the boot and struck it down into the small gash in the grass, then she led her horse towards the circle, tickling Bert's ears.

'Who *is* that?' asked Stigg.

'That's the woman that lives in that big house on Landkey Island, Stigg,' replied Penny in whispers.

'She's looking at me!'

'She's telling Bert to go back to you! Don't worry. She's not coming over here. Those scary old druids are going to talk to her.'

Chapter Twenty-One

Live and Let Die

'My lady,' said Pyrlig, respectfully bowing his head, 'it is well that you are here. You do us a great honour.' He went on, but his second utterance was slightly less warm. 'This is my man, Belator,' he continued, turning slightly to his rear, 'Belator is…'

'Your hammer, Pyrlig. But tonight is a night for craft and subtlety. Belator will enjoy his last hours without need to show us prowess in arms, yes? Certainly, there will be no danger for him,' she added, inspecting Pyrlig's giant minder like a general appraising an army cadet. 'Good for stonework,' she said breezily. 'Other things…'

Belator didn't know quite what to say so he refused to say anything at all.

'He will not be long, he is near.'

'To whom do you refer, lady?'

'Demon. He comes soon.'

'UH OH… NOT AGAIN!' said Cai, taking his eyes off his chores as his mother and father scurried about, disconnecting taps and plugs.

'What's that, son?' asked his father Cacklog, who was stuffing the last stack of clean paper plates back into a cardboard box.

'THE BLOODY ALIEN'S COMING BACK, DAD… LOOK!'

Quetzlcarbon Yum Taxx could at least be pleased that his showbiz farewell had attracted more than a single juvenile with a can of cider. He had spun a marvellous cloud of lightning through which to manifest over a strong circular wind to rustle the long robes of the druids as impressive as anything a real UFO could have made.

He had just manifested in his finest Gold Mayan Astronaut armour and raised his golden lance when he saw Sveta Anchabadze's black hazel wand pointing directly at him. Before he could even register her intention there was a massive white flash and he passed out of existence.

Pyrlig and Belator stood gaping as the black cloud wreathed in lightning suddenly shrunk to the size of a marble. There was a loud pop and then, very slowly, the shadows began to retreat to their proper proportions. They sky became lighter and suddenly the brown flattened soil was green again. The Sorceress of Landkey mounted her horse, patted its head and left without a backward glance.

'Cai, have you been putting magic mushrooms in us teas, lad? Because if you have, me and your mother are gonna put you on the bleedin' barbecue…'

Chapter Twenty-Two

Reasons to Be Cheerful, One, Two, Three

Amie van der Kop, Clash City Record's most formidable new team member, had decided to go shopping for a vehicle to replace her black Mini 1275GT, immolated by the now-extinct Mayan demon Quetzlcarbon Yum Taxx in the car park of the Shirestones Hotel.

With fifty percent more than its true value to spend, courtesy of Brian Drake on top of her insurance payout, she was now able to contemplate a whole new class of vehicle with her South African Police severance payment banked and her direct-debit pension income payments active.

She decided to invest her two little windfalls on a mint, low-mileage LWB Land Rover, adding a headlight bar, an alarm, roof rack and a few other comforts. It was a vehicle with which she was already very familiar with back home in the bush –rugged, reliable and easier on a girl with one and a half legs than a Mini. It could also swallow more shopping than five 1275GTs and she had finally been able collect Boet, her police service dog, from quarantine in it. Amie had finally overtaken Dean and Michael in the cool stakes.

The back cargo space was the ideal den for Boet's comfy new bed and a place far away from any Yorkshireman's testicles, a snack that he had been unable to resist on at least two occasions in Pretoria.

It was time for her to move on from the retail record business in England and get into something more suited to her skills and temperament, knocking people off their feet with her new business partner Val Metcalfe, the most frightening lady doorwoman in North Yorkshire.

She had handed in her notice at Clash City Records, and to show her former employers she had no ill feeling towards them for destroying her Mini she had negotiated a settlement between Brian and his former steroid customers to stop them killing him.

Somebody else was happy too. He had a new squash racket, peace of mind and the security of a dull but lucrative future in conveyancing, petty local boundary disputes, contract law and the preparation of wills.

It was a lot less dangerous than conjuring demons and dodging vindictive druids. Had he been asked if there really were such things he would have replied thus: 'Yes. There are.'

'And don't…'

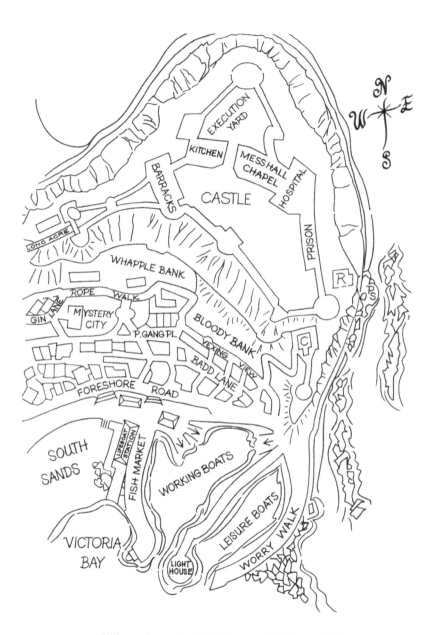

Whitborough on Sea Old Town and Harbour, 1983

Whitborough on Sea

Principal street index

Alahand St
Andrews Avenue
Badd Lane
Bramcote Lane
Beeley Avenue
Barker Row
Bleake Passage
Baldwin Terrace
Chanters Rd
Chingswell St
Cooper St
Cordon Row
Cosh Lane
Dowding Parade
Dead Man's Walk
Dark Entries Walk
Emery Row
Egg Lane
Eileifr Gate
Fawlty Row
Foster Terrace
Golf Links Rd
Gin Lane
Gracious St
Gledhill Avenue
Harris Terrace

Hawker Hurricane
    Square
Higher Gunstone
Hatchett Square
Hardy Row
Kay Row
Kingsley Rd
Knowles Terrace
Lower Gunstone
Late Lane
Littleshaw Lane
Leather Lane
Limers Lane
Long Acre
Laurel Row
Lanham Avenue
Marshall Avenue
Meddon St
Mill St
Market Square
Mallory Parade
Northdown Rd
Ogmundarson Gate
Passions Place
Plantagenet Place
Pratchett Place

Parsleysage St
Pitt Lane
Raper Avenue
Rope Walk
Samples Terrace
Swinbrook Rd
Sigurd Gate
Silver St
Tuthill Vale
Tittle Tattle Close
Tipsy Gate
Thumping Gate
The Crescent
Venerable View
Vines Square
Vexing View
Wilson Terrace
Wray Terrace
Witches Walk
White Court
Waterloo Walk
Wanderers Passage
Wyck'd Tree
Whapple Bank
Whelping Way
Whispering Gate